"It's Jack's birth certificate. This is good news, isn't it?"

"Look at the line for parents' names."

She read from the document. "Mother, Paula Ann Schulman. Father, unknown. Oh, Seth…"

The look of sympathy in her eyes wrapped around him, chasing away the sharp edges of his disappointment. When she reached out and grasped his forearm with her small hand, the warmth of her touch spread through him like a warm summer breeze.

"I'm sorry. I was hoping this would be the answer you needed."

He took her hand in his, gently squeezing her fingers. "Me, too. Now I'll have to wait on the DNA results."

"When is that due?"

"Not for a few more weeks." He looked into her sky blue eyes and realized he didn't want to break the contact. Carrie abruptly looked away and tugged her hand from his.

He shifted his position slightly, though it did nothing to diminish his acute awareness of her softness or her beauty.

Lorraine Beatty was raised in Columbus, Ohio, but now calls Mississippi home. She and her husband, Joe, have two sons and five grandchildren. Lorraine started writing in junior high and is a member of RWA and ACFW, as well as a charter member and past president of Magnolia State Romance Writers. In her spare time she likes to work in her garden, travel and spend time with her family.

Books by Lorraine Beatty

Love Inspired

Home to Dover

Protecting the Widow's Heart
His Small-Town Family
Bachelor to the Rescue
Her Christmas Hero
The Nanny's Secret Child
A Mom for Christmas
The Lawman's Secret Son

Rekindled Romance
Restoring His Heart

The Lawman's Secret Son

Lorraine Beatty

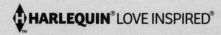

LOVE INSPIRED BOOKS

ISBN-13: 978-0-373-62259-7

The Lawman's Secret Son

www.Harlequin.com

Printed in U.S.A.

But you, Lord, do not be far from me.
You are my strength; come quickly to help me.
—*Psalms* 22:19

To my grandchildren, Drew, Anna, Addie, Casie and Chey. You are my most precious treasure.

Acknowledgments

Chaz McClain, director of children and family ministries at Lakeside Presbyterian EPC Church in Brandon, Mississippi, for his help in steering me in the right direction with my heroine's job. Your help made all the difference and is greatly appreciated.

Chapter One

Carrie Fletcher quickened her steps across the walkway from the carport to the back door of her little cottage, inserted the key and stepped into her warmly lit kitchen. She never tired of coming home to this sweet little 1920s house. The soft glow from the lights under the cabinets kept the darkness at bay and welcomed her like a warm hug, as did the click of little claws on the tile floor as her five-year-old shih tzu, Leo, scurried to greet her. "Hey, sweetie. Were you a good boy today?"

After placing her purse and a sack of groceries on the table, she flipped the switch, bathing the kitchen in full light, instantly aware of the tension falling away from her shoulders. A long and hectic day had kept her at work until dark. Her job as Special Events Coordinator at Peace Community Church was both exhilarating and challenging. Especially now, when the historic edifice was celebrating 125 years as a house of God. The yearlong celebration would culminate with a huge citywide picnic at Friendship Park. Organizing such a massive event was keeping her busy every moment.

Tomorrow was her day off and she planned on taking full advantage by sleeping late and curling up with the book she was reading. The hero and heroine had been torn apart by a terrible disaster, and she couldn't wait to see how they got back together.

A rush of happiness buoyed her spirits as she made her way through the small dining room and living room, turning up lights as she went and sending up a grateful prayer for her new life. She had a job she loved and a home of her own. She didn't own it, but her savings were growing and one day she hoped to purchase a house.

She flipped the dead bolt on the front door and switched on the porch light, which popped, then went out, surrounding her in darkness. Her throat tightened. Inhaling a deep breath, she scolded herself for being such a wimp. Her mailbox was right outside the door. She'd only be in the dark for a second or two. After opening the door, she stepped out onto the porch. Movement on the other side of the rocker froze her in her tracks. The shadows made it hard to identify the shape. A dog? Cat? A man?

Heart pounding, she peered closer. The creature scooted backward. She froze, blood pounding in her ears. She fought the impulse to duck back inside. What if it was an injured animal? She couldn't ignore that. Carrie forced herself to look closer. Two wide eyes looked back at her from a little face. A child. A little boy was huddled on her front porch. Fear slid quickly into concern. What was he doing here? Her mind raced through a dozen questions. She took a step toward the child. He scooted back against the wall, clutching a plastic grocery bag in his hands.

Slowly she stooped down, putting a smile on her face and keeping her voice calm and soothing. "Hello. My name is Carrie. What's your name?" The big eyes blinked back at her.

The boy, whom she guessed to be about five years old, didn't respond, only clutched his bag to his chest. "Are you cold? Hungry? Would you like a cookie?" He nodded. Carrie extended her hand, but he was reluctant to take it. "It's okay. I'll fix you some milk, too. Or how about hot chocolate? It's chilly tonight." It was late March in Mississippi and while the days were warming up, the evenings could still be very cold.

Slowly the child extended his hand and together they stood. When he lowered his precious sack, she saw a large note pinned to his chest. She prayed it held some answers.

The blazing lights inside her home calmed her racing pulse, and she made a mental note to replace the porch light as soon as she could. Leo greeted them, tail wagging rapidly. The boy stopped. "This is Leo. You can pet him if you'd like. He's a good boy."

The child only stared at her a moment, then backed away from the animal.

Guiding the boy toward her breakfast table, she reached for his sack, but he clutched it more tightly against his chest. She noticed he held a toy in his other hand, a small yellow truck, battered and bent with much

of the paint worn away and a tire missing from one
of the wheels. A long-ago memory exhumed itself. A
shiny blue bracelet. The only thing that had ever belonged to her. She'd lost it somewhere along the way,
but she'd cherished it much the same way the little boy
did his truck.

Settling him onto a chair, she briefly rested her hand
on the top of his head, surprised at how cool he felt.
How long had he been on her porch? The thin jacket he
wore was woefully inadequate for the weather. His jeans
were threadbare and his sneakers worn through at the
toes. Her heart ballooned with sympathy. She wanted
to wrap him in her arms and make him warm and safe,
but she doubted he'd let her do that.

She heated up a cup of water in the microwave, added
a packet of cocoa, took two cookies from the jar and
set them in front of the boy before joining him. "I see
you have a note. It must be important. May I see it?"

He thought a moment, then nodded. Carrie unpinned
the stained and crumpled paper. It was folded in half
with the number 533 scribbled on it. As she read the
short note inside, a swell of familiar anger formed.

Seth, I'm done. He's your son and it's time you
did your part. He's five years old. Do the math.
I'm leaving the country. His name is Jack. Tiff

Seth. That was the name of her new neighbor, the
man who had so kindly changed her flat tire last week.
She'd labeled him a good guy—kind, charming and
nice. She'd even felt a spark of attraction to his solid

strength and boy-next-door smile. Apparently there was another side to the man—deadbeat dad. She would never understand how a man could father a child, then walk away. Still, she found it hard to believe Seth was that kind of man. It was a shame. He'd been so thoughtful and seemed so trustworthy. But then she was a terrible judge of character.

Carrie scanned the note once more, making sure she hadn't missed something. Nope. The boy was Seth's, and for whatever reason he'd been left on her doorstep. Well, this was a situation she was *not* going to get involved in. She watched Jack sipping the cocoa and taking small bites of the cookies as if wanting the experience to last. Her throat constricted. She knew that feeling. Memories, hot and stinging, shot through her system. She ached to hold the child and make sure he never felt this way again. But Jack wasn't her responsibility. He was Seth's.

Jack downed the last of his milk, wiped his sleeve across his little mouth, then stared at her. She forced a smile. "Jack. Do you know who left you here? Your mom, grandma or a friend?"

He stared back at her with the biggest cobalt blue eyes she'd ever seen. No. She'd seen them once before. Seth's eyes were the same color. Only his eyes had crinkles at the corners and a warm, friendly light in them that drew people in.

Focus. She fingered the note again. "Jack, I think you've been left here by mistake. You should be next door. That's where your...father lives. How about we go see him?"

Jack shrugged his bony shoulders and her throat tightened. The poor little guy was lost and afraid. From deep down, old hurts and fears coalesced into a ball of fury. This was the reason she was taking online classes to become a social worker. She vowed to help kids feel safe and protected. The way she'd never been. Part of her wanted to call the authorities, but the note clearly was intended for her neighbor and that's where she would start.

Leo put his paws on Jack's chair and whined. Jack reached down cautiously and touched the top of the dog's brown-and-white head. Carrie wasn't sure but she thought she heard a small giggle. The sound shot straight to her core, wrapping around her like a fast-growing kudzu vine. She stood. Time to get a grip, before she became more attached to the little fellow.

Holding on to Jack's small hand, she walked across the front lawn and up onto Seth's front porch. It was dark, the only light coming from deep inside the cottage. A chill chased up her spine. *You are my strength.* Darkness had never been her friend. But this wasn't about her. This was about Jack. She would explain the mix-up, hand the boy over and be on her way. This was none of her concern. She smiled down at Jack and knocked firmly on the door. Very firmly.

The door swung open, and the outline of a man back-lit from inside filled the doorway. He stood braced with feet apart. She swallowed a sudden lump in her throat. She'd forgotten how tall her neighbor was and how broad his shoulders were. In the shadowed light he seemed imposing. Her heart skipped a beat. Would he scare Jack?

The porch light flipped on and Seth met her gaze with a questioning frown. "Carrie? Hey. What brings you by tonight?" He glanced down at the child, his frown sliding into a curious smile. "Who's your little friend?"

Carrie clenched her teeth. Really? The man didn't even know his own son? This is why she'd vowed to steer clear of any romantic entanglements. Men were all totally irresponsible and self-absorbed. No matter how nice they might seem in the beginning, they would leave you in the end.

"He's your son. But I guess not seeing him for a long time might make him hard to recognize." She hadn't intended to react in anger, but his indifference had sparked a nerve.

The warm smile vanished, replaced with a look of stunned shock before the dark brows drew together and the eyes narrowed. "I don't know what kind of joke you're playing, Carrie, but it isn't funny."

"No, it's anything *but* funny. It's tragic and irresponsible and unforgivable."

Seth placed a hand on the doorjamb, leaning toward her, his scowl slightly threatening. "I don't have a son. I'm not even married."

Carrie rolled her eyes and, stooping down, gently turned Jack to face her. "This is your father, Jack. He's going to take good care of you, okay?" Unable to stop herself, she gave him a hug, then angled him to face Seth and gave the boy a nudge forward. "He's already had hot chocolate and cookies at my house, but you might want to fix him something nourishing to eat." She tried not to glare in disgust but failed. "Good night." She pivoted and started down the steps.

"Carrie."

Jack ran after her, grabbing on to her hand for dear life. She looked down into his frightened eyes and her heart broke. "Oh, Jack. It'll be all right. I promise." She glanced up at Seth, who had stepped to the edge of the porch. The look on his face tugged at her heart, too. It was an unusual mixture of concern, longing and fear. Maybe he was telling the truth. Maybe he didn't know about Jack. As she considered the possibility, Seth came and stooped down with them.

"Hey, Jack. Why don't we all go inside and get warm, huh?"

With only a hint of hesitancy, Seth gently touched the child's head before looking at Carrie with a pleading look in his eyes. It was the last thing she wanted to do, but she couldn't simply turn the child over to the man without making sure Jack was okay. But she shouldn't get involved. Her emotions were too easily captured by the abandoned and abused. She would have to keep her emotional guard up. She nodded and stood, holding on to the tiny hand. It hit her that she was looking to the child for strength when it should be the other way around. At the threshold Carrie stopped, sending a quick prayer heavenward for strength, because she had a feeling stepping into Seth's home would set her on a path she'd avoided most of her life. Jack looked up at her with soulful eyes.

She'd be strong for Jack because no one understood what he was feeling like she did. She had no choice but to step inside.

Seth stood aside as his guests entered, the knot in his chest pressing so fiercely against his ribs it ached to draw breath. His thoughts darted in a dozen directions, trying to grasp something logical about Carrie's announcement. The boy couldn't possibly be his. He closed the door and moved to the living room, making a quick assessment of his lovely neighbor. She'd seemed nice and sweet the day he'd found her crouched down beside her small car staring at the deflated tire. Now he took a closer look. Was she a con artist? A mental case? It was his nature to question things, especially people. She didn't look like she had a devious bone in her body. In fact, with her slender frame, her short, blond, feathery hair style and bright blue eyes she evoked thoughts of summer and sunshine. But as a cop he knew everyone had a dark side.

He rubbed his forehead. "Have a seat."

Reluctantly, Carrie sat on the sofa, pulling the boy down beside her. The child had released Carrie's hand, but his hand was now firmly wrapped around a toy he'd pulled from his pocket. The old Tonka truck looked like it had been through a war. In his other hand he grasped a dirty plastic grocery sack.

Seth stood near the fireplace facing the pair, taking a position of authority. "Now, you want to explain what's going on here? What makes you think the boy is mine?"

Carrie pulled a paper from her pocket and handed it

to him. "I'm sure this will clear everything up for you. It was pinned to his chest when I found him on my porch a short while ago."

"What?" He took the note and read through it, his mind refusing to grasp the words. This couldn't be happening. It couldn't be true. Not now, when he was finally making things right in his life. A lump of old shame and regret formed in his gut. He was a Montgomery. The son of a prominent and well-respected family in Dover. But he'd turned his back on his heritage and his values for a year of freedom that had quickly become a life of darkness and regret. Now that shameful time might have finally caught up with him.

He looked at Carrie, and the condemnation in her blue eyes stung. "I don't understand any of this. And why was he left on your porch?"

She pointed to the number on the back of the paper he held, lowering her voice so Jack couldn't hear. "Five thirty-three. That's your house number. Mine is five thirty-five. I think whoever left him thought they were leaving him on your porch."

That tidbit of information latched on to him like the talons of a hawk. "Tiff was dyslexic." He muttered the words to himself, but Carrie pounced on them.

"So she thought she was leaving him on your porch. Who's Tiff?"

The scorn in her voice shot his defenses into place. "My ex-wife. We were only married a short time." *Short* was being generous. Six weeks, two days and four hours, to be exact.

"Perhaps you should call her for an explanation." Carrie stood and started for the door.

"I haven't seen or heard from her in years. She never told me about…" He looked at the child, who had scooted onto the floor and was playing quietly with the battered truck.

Carrie crossed her arms over her chest, her expression clearly revealing her skepticism. "So you're saying she kept the child a secret from you? Why would she do that?"

Good question. He put his fists on his hips. "I don't know."

He looked at the child again, so small and frail. Could the boy be his son? Somewhere deep inside, a feeling began to form. It wouldn't be out of character for Tiff to have kept her pregnancy a secret. She'd thought she was marrying a fun guy who could keep her in high style. But when the money had run out, so had she. But why bring the boy to him now and abandon him on the porch? That was heartless even for her.

He ran his hands down his face, staring at Jack. "This is crazy. I don't understand any of it." The note said the boy was five. He'd done the math. It added up. A father. He'd never considered that. At least not for a long time. His foray into the Vegas lifestyle had drawn out all of his sinful nature, and he'd spent the last years trying to overcome it. Was it true? Was Jack his?

Carrie cleared her throat softly. "Seth, do you have something good for Jack to eat?"

Seth frowned. Was she kidding? His life had been upended and she was wondering about food? One glance at the child banished his irritation. He didn't know a lot about children, but it didn't take much to see the boy was thin and sallow-looking, and his cobalt blue eyes were set too deeply in his face, as if he might have been hungry awhile.

His eyes. Seth's heart skipped a beat and that feeling deep inside grew stronger. The cobalt color was a Montgomery family trait. The only one of his siblings who didn't have them was his sister Bethany, who'd inherited their grandmother's hazel color. He glanced at Carrie. She was looking at him with expectancy. Food. Right. "Uh, like what? Cold pizza? Lunch meat?"

"Fruit or cereal, perhaps?"

He winced at her scolding tone. "Right." He moved into the kitchen. Good food. Nourishing food. Things he rarely purchased. All he could scrounge up was a slightly overripe banana.

"Will this work?"

Carried arched her brows as she urged Jack to his feet. "Jack, let's get you over to your dad's table and you can play with your truck while you eat this. We'll be right here where you can see us, okay?"

After settling Jack at the table, Carrie approached Seth, her blue eyes wary and concerned.

"Seth, what's going on? Is he yours or not?"

"I don't know. Maybe. It's possible. I have to figure out what I'm going to do with him."

"You're not thinking of sending him to foster care, are you? You can't. He'll be just a number there with no one to comfort him."

Seth frowned. "I only meant I need to find someone to take care of Jack while I'm at work. I just finished orientation for my new job. I need to show them I'm committed and dependable. I can't do that if I keep taking off work to watch Jack." That wasn't the only thing he was concerned about. Jack's sudden appearance would stir up gossip. He didn't want his family paying for his past mistakes.

"What about friends and family? I know you just moved here, but are they close by?"

Seth shook his head. "Moved *back* here. I grew up in Dover. My family has lived here for generations. Everyone knows us. But I can't ask them for help."

Carrie put her hand to her throat. "Wait. Montgomery. Are you one of *those* Montgomerys? Montgomery Real Estate, Montgomery Electrical Contractors and the woman who has the event planning business?"

"Yes. Why?"

"So why don't you want to ask them for help?"

"I need time to sort this out and look into things and see if this child is really mine. I can't just take the word of some faded paper. There's no point in upsetting my family until I know more." Embarrassing them was closer to the truth. In a town the size of Dover, an unexplained child could start tongues wagging.

"I suppose. But they're your family. Don't they deserve to know what's going on?"

"My family knows nothing about that time in my life."

"Why not?"

He took a moment to collect his thoughts. It wasn't a topic he liked to think about, let alone discuss. "Let's just say I was the rebel of the clan. I was never content in Dover, so I left and moved to Las Vegas. Eventually I came to my senses and the end of my finances, and I came home."

"The prodigal son. And that's when you got married?"

"One of my big mistakes. I'm not proud of that time in my life, and I've spent years trying to put it behind me."

Carrie stiffened her neck. "And an unexpected child now would be awkward. Even scandalous."

"Yes. It would. Especially since I'm starting a new job. But first I have to find out the truth about this boy and why he was dumped here without any word."

"So what are you going to do?"

"Try to find his mother. She's the only one with answers."

"And Jack?"

He glanced at the boy before facing Carrie. "I'll take care of him until we get to the bottom of this." Her blue eyes lightened in relief. Had she expected him to toss the boy out again? Did she think he was the kind of man who would walk away from his child? He couldn't blame her given the cryptic note she'd read. She'd probably pegged him as a deadbeat dad.

She stood and started toward the door. The long blue skirt she wore swished attractively below the soft white blouse, making him think of clouds in a summer sky. He shut down the thought. "Where are you going? You can't leave yet."

"I can and I am. This is not my problem. I brought him safely to you. Now I'm going home."

"Carrie."

Jack ran out of the kitchen, traces of banana on his mouth. "Don't go."

She stooped down and hugged him. "It's okay, Jack. I'll be right next door if you need me. You can see my house from that window. I'll wave to you when I get home, okay?" She shot a warning glare in Seth's direction.

Jack's mouth puckered up and he nodded. "Leo?"

She led him to the window. "He'll wave, too. Now you stand right here, and as soon as I get inside I'll wave at you."

The thought of being alone with the little boy suddenly filled him with terror. "Carrie, are you sure you can't stay awhile? I could really use your help."

"I'm positive." She opened the door. "And, Seth, be gentle with him, okay? He needs to feel safe and loved whether he's yours or not."

Her warning triggered his curiosity. Why was she so protective of a child she didn't know? She seemed very knowledgeable about how Jack felt and what he needed. He had a feeling she was coming from a place of experience. Assessing people was part of his job and one of his gifts. He wanted to know more about the intriguing Carrie Fletcher.

She stopped at the threshold and glanced over her shoulder. "Oh, and, Seth, he needs a bath before you put him to bed."

Her stern expression reminded him of the disapprov-

ing looks he'd gotten from his teachers when he'd mis-
behaved. He watched her start across the lawn, then
realized his major mistake. "Carrie. Thanks for taking
care of Jack." She looked over her shoulder, her blond
hair catching the light from the streetlamp.

"Make sure you take care of him or I *will* call the
cops." If he hadn't been so shell-shocked he would have
laughed at her threat. But she had a point. He needed
to get to the bottom of this and find out the truth about
the little boy. A father. The possibility was both scary
and intriguing.

He started formulating a plan as he went back inside. He needed the truth and he needed it fast, before
everything in his life started to unravel.

Safely inside her cottage again, Carrie scooped up
Leo, went to the window facing Seth's house and raised
the fabric shade. She could see Jack's little face pressed
against the glass and his hand waving frantically. Behind him a shadow moved. Seth? She waved until the
boy disappeared from view, her heart pinching. Had she
done the right thing in leaving him there?

Had there been another option? The rest was up to
Seth to figure out. In the kitchen she put away the groceries, filled a bowl with leftover casserole and set it
to heat in the microwave. Leo followed her to the bedroom, where she changed into a pair of sweatpants and
a loose T-shirt. Friday night was movie night and she
had every intention of keeping to her routine.

But her thoughts kept replaying the expression on
Seth's face. She'd been furious with the man, but not

so upset that she hadn't seen the color drain from his face as he read the note.

She'd expected continued denial, even anger, but he'd been more stunned and confused than anything. He'd stared at Jack as if he were an alien creature. But he'd also spoken gently to him, and she'd seen a glint of compassion in his eyes. At least he hadn't thrown her and Jack out.

Her instincts told her Seth had been telling the truth. He hadn't known about Jack. He'd even shared about his less-than-noble life in Vegas. Yet he was doing the right thing in keeping Jack and at the same time trying not to bring shame on his family.

She wandered to the window and peeked over at Seth's house again. The window was dark. Had they gone to bed? Had he tucked Jack in? Given him a bath? After grabbing the cord beside the window, she lowered the shade and turned away. Out of sight, out of mind. She had to let this go. Jack was Seth's responsibility now.

Her cell phone rang and she picked it up, surprised to see Kathy Edwards's name on the screen. What would she be calling for? The supervisor of the church preschool was a good friend and coworker. But with two small children and a husband, they rarely spoke outside of the office.

"Sorry to disturb your evening, Carrie, but I wanted to let you know I found a volunteer to take charge of the games the day of the picnic."

"Wonderful. Who?"

"Earl Michaels. Turns out he used to work for his

uncle's carnival growing up and he says he knows all about managing several events at once."

Carrie chuckled at the image forming in her mind of the dapper Mr. Michaels barking for a carnival. "That leaves only two more spots to fill."

"Yep. However, I have to tell you, I ran into Ralph as I was leaving and he forgot to take the flyer to the printers today, and now we won't have them to hand out at church on Sunday."

Carrie sank down onto the sofa. "Great. I really wanted those available this weekend. What happened?"

"He claims we never gave the original to him. Carrie, I know Ralph has been the go-to guy for the church forever and he prides himself on being an unofficial assistant to every church event, but he's getting older and forgetful and he doesn't hear as well as he should."

Carrie knew only too well. Ralph had pledged his help for the Chili Cook-Off last month, but she'd ended up doing everything herself, taking valuable time away from other projects because Ralph either didn't show up or confused his instructions.

"I think we need to make an announcement for a new assistant."

"And break Ralph's heart? Not to mention humiliating him. I can't do that." Ralph had a heart as big as all outdoors and he loved his Lord and his church. He would never understand being replaced.

"Carrie, you need someone to help you. You're stretched to the max now."

"I know. We'll have to pray that the Lord will provide the perfect solution."

"I wish I had your faith. All I see is a worn-out friend who's going to crumble into dust once this picnic is over."

"Then I'll count on you to bring me hot soup and chocolate cake."

They discussed a few more issues with the picnic before hanging up. Carrie was continually amazed at how the Lord had worked through her life, bestowing blessings that she never dreamed possible. He'd taken the battered, confused and hurting person she'd been, restored her and made her whole again. Her life was finally moving in the right direction. She had a decent education, a job that paid a comfortable wage and a work environment that not only made her happy but fed her spiritually, as well.

Now she was free to save up for her house and finish her degree. One by one she was conquering the shadows of her childhood and sealing them up as securely as the record of her past.

Or was that really the truth? Seth's past had revisited him tonight. Would hers do the same? Would it rise up like a dark fist and smash her new world to pieces again? She shook her head to dislodge the negative thoughts. Her past followed her around like Marley's chain. She'd tried to forget it, to ignore it, but she couldn't let it go even though she knew deep down she wasn't that person anymore. She was a child of God—loved, worthy and valued. He'd set her on a new path, and looking back wouldn't gain her anything. She had to trust that He would sort it all out. But it wouldn't hurt to keep her guard up and her heart protected.

Chapter Two

Seth stared at the small boy playing with the battered yellow truck. He'd reread the note a dozen times, looking for something he'd missed, and had spent the last half hour making calls that had gotten him nowhere. There was no number listed in Vegas for his former wife, and the few contacts he still had proved to be dead ends. A quick search on the internet had been fruitless, too. He couldn't take the note at face value, but something inside him knew that the words were true. He simply wasn't ready to accept it without investigating. He needed a birth certificate, proof of some sort that Jack was his. He needed access to the police department files, but as a newbie on the Dover force he didn't have many favors to call in. He'd have to wait until he reported to work on Monday and see what he could accomplish.

Right now he had a more pressing task to address—telling his mother about Jack. He needed to do that soon. It wouldn't take but a moment for word to get out, and he didn't want her to learn about his son from strangers or rumors. Telling his siblings was another thing he wasn't looking forward to. He had to uncover the truth for everyone's sake.

His attention returned to the little boy sitting in front of the hearth. Their gazes collided, sending a jolt of recognition along Seth's nerves. Those big cobalt blue eyes were better than any birth certificate.

The boy looked uneasy, forcing Seth to realize that since Carrie had left he'd been preoccupied with phone calls and internet searches instead of paying attention to Jack. That was something he'd have to correct.

He leaned forward, opening his arms and offering his best smile. "Hey, Jack. Come over here. Let me see that cool truck of yours." The boy hesitated only a moment before standing and coming to him. He stopped within the circle of Seth's body, and he was struck again by how small and frail the child was. His throat tightened. Jack was a baby. Too young to be abandoned by the one who should love him most. Seth sent up a grateful prayer that Carrie had been the person to find him and that Jack was now safe with him.

"That's a really sharp looking truck you have, buddy."

"It's a supertruck."

Seth smiled at the sincere look in his blue eyes. It was the most Jack had said all evening. He hoped that meant he was feeling more comfortable. "Awesome. What does it do?"

Jack fingered the battered toy. "It can fly." He angled the toy into the air. "It can go way faster than anything."

"That's cool."

A frown tugged his little brows downward. "What's your name?"

The simple question hit with the force of a sledge-hammer to his solar plexus. That was the biggest question of his life. What did he tell the child? While his instincts said Jack was his son, if he was wrong it would be wise to keep some emotional distance for both their sakes. He searched for a compromise. "My name is Seth, but how about you call me Pop?"

Jack thought a moment, then smiled. "That's a silly name."

He picked Jack up and set him on his lap. "It's what we used to call my dad. It's sort of a special nickname."

"Are you my dad?"

The longing in the little voice tore through him. He pulled the boy closer. "We're going to figure that out together, okay?" The odor from his dirty clothing assaulted Seth's nose.

Carrie had pointed out that he needed a bath. It was after eight o'clock. Time for Jack to be asleep. Reaching for the plastic sack, Seth pulled out what he hoped were clean clothes but proved to be little more than rags. His shoes had holes in the toes, the thin T-shirt was useless and there was no clean underwear at all. How could Tiff have treated the boy this way? She'd had her problems, but he'd never imagined her as an unfit mother. Who was he kidding? He didn't know anything about his former wife. That was the problem.

His problem now was what to do with Jack. The clothes he wore would probably disintegrate in the washer. This was a bachelor household. He'd only been back in Dover a few weeks, and he'd been too busy getting settled into his house and his new role as a Dover police officer to think of much else.

He needed help. Seth rubbed his forehead. There was only one person he could turn to, and he dreaded asking. A glance at the clock pointed out how late it was. Jack needed to go to bed. He picked up his phone and dialed Carrie's number. "Hey, Carrie."

"Seth? Is Jack okay? What's wrong?"

"Jack's fine, but I need your help." He could sense her resistance through the connection. He hoped she wouldn't turn him down. "I went through the things in Jack's bag. None of the clothes are wearable, and the ones he has on should be tossed. I want to give him a bath, but I don't have anything for him to put on afterward. I thought maybe you had a small shirt or something."

"No, nothing that tiny. I'll be right over."

She was at the door within moments, and clearly unhappy to be there. She'd changed from the simple skirt and top she'd worn earlier to dark sweatpants and a T-shirt with a faded logo on the front. She looked younger, more approachable. Jack ran and hugged her, a big smile lighting his face. Seth's concern eased a bit. Carrie would know what to do. "Any suggestions?"

"You'll have to go shopping."

"Now? Where? It's Friday night in Dover. Every place is closed."

"Not all. The Dollar General is open. They'll have everything you need. I'll stay here and give Jack his bath."

Seth ran a hand down the back of his neck. He didn't

know what he'd expected, but shopping hadn't entered the picture. "I don't know anything about what a kid needs."

"He needs the same things you do, only in smaller sizes. For now we'll guess at those. Probably size 4." Carrie scribbled on a piece of paper and handed it to him. "He'll need pj's, jeans, T-shirts, shoes and socks, underwear and a jacket."

"All that to go to bed?"

"He can't wear pajamas all the time."

She looked at him as if he was the dumbest man on the planet. And he was when it came to kids. "Right." He scanned the list. It seemed simple enough, but he'd rather stay and give Jack his bath and let her go to the store. But he didn't know anything about that, either.

"Okay. I'll be back as soon as I can." He grabbed his jacket and started for the door.

"Seth, add a toothbrush to your list. And maybe a stuffed animal."

He wasn't sure why the toy had been added, but he nodded and opened the door. He stopped, glancing over his shoulder. "Thanks, Carrie. I really appreciate your help."

"I'm doing this for Jack."

Her tone clearly showed her displeasure with him. Did she still have him pegged as a deadbeat dad? He didn't like being seen that way. He'd have to change her mind and show her that he wasn't that kind of man, though why her opinion should matter left him puzzled. She wasn't even his type. He'd always been drawn to the tall, dark, sultry types, with long hair and even longer legs. Maybe that was his problem. Maybe he should be looking for someone real, with a gentle spirit and fierce love for kids.

Except he wasn't looking for any kind of relationship. Not in the near future.

Carrie ran her fingers over Jack's soft, freshly washed hair. After his bath she'd wrapped him in a towel, and together they'd snuggled on the sofa to wait for Seth. The child was tired and the warm bath had lulled him close to sleep, but for some reason he was fighting it. Every few moments he'd glance at the door. She realized he was waiting for Seth to return and probably wouldn't sleep until he was home.

He'd already called four times with questions. What's the difference between a size 4 and a 4T? Did little boys like red or blue pj's? How did he buy shoes when he didn't know the size? And would a dog or a bear be a better stuffed toy?

She had to give him credit. He was trying. He could have easily grabbed the first thing he'd seen and dashed home.

Pulling a magazine from the small stack on the end table, she flipped to a page and began to read softly, "'When working with a lathe, it's important to keep a steady pressure on the gouge to ensure the proper depth and angle of the design. This master kit of gouge tools includes everything you'll need to create the perfect spindles, bowls and other—'"

"I never realized a woodworking catalog had bedtime-story appeal."

Carrie started when she heard Seth's voice behind her. She hadn't heard him come in, so content was she with Jack cuddled in her arms. He was a sweet little boy, starved for affection, and her heart had already lost its battle to keep her emotional distance. She wanted to keep him close and make sure he never felt abandoned again.

"It's not the words that lull them to sleep—it's being close and hearing your voice that comforts children."

"I'll try to remember that." He took a seat on the coffee table and began unloading his bounty.

Jack stirred and grinned at Seth. "Hi, Pop."

"Hi, Jack." Seth ruffled the boy's hair affectionately. "I got you some new pajamas. Let's get them on so you can go to bed."

"Pop?" Carrie shot a glance at Seth as he handed her the package of superhero briefs.

"It's what we used to call my dad. It's too soon for anything else."

Carrie pulled labels off the blue pajamas, slipping the shirt over Jack's head. Too soon? Did that mean Seth was starting to believe Jack was his?

Dressed in his new pajamas and smelling like soap, Jack looked like a very different child. There was a warmth in his eyes that hadn't been there before. She thanked the Lord for that and prayed Jack would always feel safe and loved.

"Seth, I'm going to help Jack brush his teeth. Why don't you get the bed ready?"

"Right." He disappeared down the hall.

A few moments later Carrie took Jack's hand and

walked him toward the master bedroom. Seth was seated on the edge of the bed, covers folded back and a smile on his face. A brown-and-white stuffed dog waited on the pillow. Jack let go of Carrie's hand and hurried forward.

"Leo." He took the stuffed toy and held it to his chest.

Seth frowned. Carrie hastened to explain. "It looks like my dog, Leo."

"You mean that little fuzzy rodent I see in your yard?"

Carrie sent him a disapproving glare. "What are you going to name your dog, Jack?"

The child thought for a moment. "Barky."

Seth nodded in approval as he tucked the covers around the small body and ran a gentle hand over the little head. "That's a super name. Ready to say your prayers?" Jack shrugged his shoulders. "We'll make this first one short." He folded the boy's hands together and a said a quick blessing.

The gesture caught Carrie off guard. She hadn't expected Seth to be a man of faith. Something inside her shifted, leaving an odd, uncomfortable tightening in her chest.

"Amen. See you in the morning, Jack."

"Pop? You won't go away?"

Carrie's throat constricted and she could see the tendons in Seth's neck flex with emotion. "No, Jack. I'll be right here when you wake up. Promise."

Reassured, Jack was asleep before they stepped out of the room.

As if having the same thought, they turned at the door to watch the small boy in the big bed as he slept.

Seth rested a hand against the door frame. "He looks so small."

"You should have seen him in the tub." She wrapped her arms around her waist in a vain attempt to quell the sadness inside. "Without his clothes, he's just skin and bones. It broke my heart."

"I know. I can't believe someone just dumped him on your porch and walked away."

"It happens all too often."

"You sound like you have experience in these matters."

Carrie glanced at Seth and saw the curiosity in his eyes, along with a hint of concern that warmed her. "I'm studying toward my degree in social work. There are too many children who get lost in the system. They need an advocate."

One corner of his mouth lifted, revealing a charming crease in his cheek. "Well, from what I've seen tonight, you'll make an excellent one."

His compliment brought a rush of heat to her face. She never knew how to respond when people said nice things to her, but the smile he'd given her had kicked her pulse rate up a few notches. One of the first things she'd noticed about him was his knock-you-to-your-knees smile. He had two deep creases, like elongated dimples, on either side of his mouth, and they flashed whenever he spoke. It was a fascinating face, one she could watch for hours.

She stopped her wayward thoughts and glanced back

at the sleeping boy to collect herself. Seth shifted beside her, sending a whiff of tangy aftershave in her direction.

"Contrary to what you might think, I would never abandon a child of mine. If I'd known about Jack, I would have fought to be part of his life."

She wanted to believe that. She wanted to believe that her first impression of him was the correct one. That he was a nice guy, a man of character. But how did she know for certain? Those kind of men had been absent in her life. It was easier and safer to lump them all into one negative category.

Seth must have read the doubt and confusion in her eyes. He touched her arm lightly, and the contact sent a rush of warmth along her skin, awakening another layer of awareness of the man beside her. At five feet five inches, she wasn't short, but Seth's six-foot height and solid build made her feel petite. The kindness in his eyes wrapped around her like a gentle hug.

"I'll take good care of Jack. You don't need to worry. We both care about the little guy and want what's best for him. But it's going to take some time to sort this out."

His words eased some of her concern. "I know. I just don't want him to feel alone."

"He won't. I'll be with him until we get to the bottom of this. And he has you and Leo right next door."

She wasn't sure that was a good thing. In a few short hours she'd become entangled with the little boy and drawn into Seth's life. She turned her attention back to the bed. They stood at the bedroom door watching Jack sleep, both reluctant to leave him alone. Carrie knew she should not get involved in this situation, but that resolve had already started to crumble.

"What if you can't find her?" She hated to think of what kind of future the child might face if that happened.

Seth sighed. "Let's not borrow trouble. For now let's make our little guy happy while we look for answers."

Our little guy. Their mutual affection for Jack and their desire to help him had bonded them whether she liked it or not. For the immediate future, they were his advocates. She looked into Seth's eyes and thought she read the same strength and determination there that was inside her. It would be nice to have a partner, someone equally dedicated to the cause.

A small chamber of her heart clicked open, as if suddenly unlocked after years of neglect. She fought back the swell of attraction and the need for connection swirling inside. She couldn't afford to depend on anyone, not even a man as handsome and kind as Seth. There was too much at stake in her life right now. The pressure in her chest increased, forcing her to take quick breaths. She had to get out of there. Away from Seth. She needed space and time to think.

"I'd better go." She hurried to the living room, but stopped at the front door when Seth called her name.

"You want me to check with you in the morning and let you know how Jack slept?"

No. She wanted out of this situation. A memory of Jack scared and abandoned on her porch tapped into her deep need to help. How could she refuse now that she'd become attached to the little guy? "Yes. That would be nice." With one last look at Seth, she forced herself to walk away, hurrying across the yard and not stopping until she was safely inside her home.

Curled up on her bed, she took a few deep breaths to calm her anxious mind. Leo hopped up and settled into her lap, and she buried her fingers in the soft, thick fur. Petting Leo always calmed her down. Too bad he couldn't teach her to be stronger in her convictions.

When would she learn to listen to that warning voice inside when it spoke? She'd told herself not to get involved with Jack's situation. She'd heard the warning bells before she'd stepped inside Seth's home and again when he'd called and asked for her help. But she couldn't turn away from the little boy's needs.

Dealing with Seth was another matter. Her unexpected attraction to Seth was disturbing. She had closed the door on relationships long ago. She'd seen firsthand how letting your heart rule your head always led to disaster. Especially when you had a past that needed to stay buried.

The memory of Jack snuggled in her arms, his head tucked under her chin as she read the magazine, tapped into a longing she didn't allow herself to contemplate. A child of her own, a home, a husband. A life she wasn't entitled to. But, for one second, as they'd stood watching Jack sleep, both of them so full of affection for the boy, it had been as if they were Mom and Dad tucking their child into bed.

That was a life she'd never have. The legacy of her childhood wasn't something she would inflict on anyone. Not a husband and certainly not a child. No one would understand her childhood or the things she'd done to survive. But that was long ago. She was a different person now. A woman with a renewed mind and heart. She'd accepted the fact that spending her life alone was the price for that transformation, and she didn't regret it. She had more blessings than she could count, and she would thank the Lord every day of her life.

God had given her a mission to devote herself to helping children trapped in bad situations. She would be their champion the way Mavis Tanner had been hers. Another year of classes and she'd have her degree. All she had to do was stay focused.

She scooted under the covers, tugging them up to her chin and holding Leo tight in her arms. She couldn't afford to be distracted by a lovable little boy and a man with eyes filled with warmth and tenderness.

Carrie took another bite of her cereal, the hungry birds gathered around the feeder outside her breakfast-room window providing her morning entertainment. She'd slept late because she'd spent most of the night replaying last night's events over in her mind.

She'd finally fallen asleep, but even her dreams had been filled with images of being alone, lost in the dark and being chased down shadowed rain-slicked streets. All old subconscious fears born of her own troubled past.

Still, she couldn't help wondering how Jack had fared after they'd settled him in bed last night. Glancing out the window again, she saw Seth and Jack walking toward the truck. The group of cottages where she lived was known as Collinstown, built by a former logging company in the 1920s to house their employees. The driveways were positioned off an alleyway in the back, leaving the front yards facing the tree-lined streets and the park in the center of the little neighborhood.

Her insides warmed as she watched the man and child. Jack was still holding his metal truck tightly in his hand, but Seth held the other. She wondered where they were going this morning.

A jolt of realization seized her chest. She darted through the door and jogged across the lawn. "Seth. What are you doing?" Breathless, she stopped at the fence. Jack, already in the backseat of the cab, waved at her from the window.

Seth's dark brows arched when he looked at her. "We're going to pick up a few things."

"But he needs a car seat."

A muscle in his jaw flexed, then his mouth lifted at one corner. "Well, I checked the cupboard and I was fresh out of kids' car seats. Unless you have one I could borrow?"

"Of course not. I don't have kids."

He leaned toward her, a sardonic grin on his face. "Neither did I. Until last night."

Jack waved at her from the window of the truck and pointed downward. Leo had come outside to join them. "But you have to keep him safe."

Crossing his arms over his chest, he nodded thoughtfully. "I considered letting him ride in the truck bed, but it's too cold for that."

"You can't be serious…" The smirk on his face stopped her protest.

He grinned and took a step closer. "Stop worrying. I'm going to strap him nice and tight in the backseat, drive very carefully to the store and get him a car seat. Is that the right answer?"

Her cheeks warmed and she took a step back. "Sorry. I just don't want anything to happen to Jack. He's been through enough."

"I know." Seth's tender gaze caused a skip in her pulse.

"And after that?"

"We're going shopping for clothes that fit. And a bed."

"You're going to keep him?"

Seth's expression grew serious and he nodded, rubbing his chin. "Just until I can get him to a little-boy shelter where he can find a good home."

Hot emotion burst through her system. "What kind of heartless man are you?"

Seth raised his palms. "Easy. I'm just kidding. I'm sorry. I didn't know it would upset you so much. You take things too seriously. Of course I'm keeping him. At least until I know exactly what's going on. I told you that last night."

Carrie tugged at the strand of hair near her ear. "I know, but things can change."

"I don't go back on my word, Carrie. Jack's not going anywhere until we sort this all out. Trust me on that."

She wanted to believe him, but the skeptical part of her ran deep. For now, she'd give him the benefit of the doubt until he proved her wrong. Then she'd be there to take charge of Jack. "Okay, then." She backed away from the fence. "Be sure and check that the shoes you buy have at least an inch between his toe and the end of the shoe. And he really needs a warmer jacket." Jack waved again. And she waved back, unable to keep from smiling. He looked excited. "And maybe a haircut?"

"Maybe what he really needs is a friend to come along and help."

Was he asking her to join them? Out of the question. This was just what she'd worried about. Getting drawn into the problem. She'd been in that situation several times, and it always ended with her heart being broken. "Oh. No. I'm sure you'll do fine. The store clerks will help you find what he needs."

Seth cocked an eyebrow. "He asked about you this morning. He went to the front window several times, hoping to see you and wave."

"He did?" The thought warmed her. She'd thought about it several times and decided against it.

"Carrie, honestly, I really could use your help. I'm out of my comfort zone here."

Her gaze drifted to Jack, his little smile climbing inside her heart and taking root. She wanted to make sure he had what he needed. "Okay. Give me a few minutes to change."

Once again she ignored the voice telling her to stay home and mind her own business. But she had to admit that spending time with Jack was appealing. As far as Seth was concerned, that was a different problem. She stopped at her back door and glanced back. Seth was leaning against the truck, looking good in his dark jeans and a deep blue cotton shirt rolled up at the sleeves. He could have been posing for an advertisement.

Nope. This was not good...at all.

Chapter Three

A short while later, settled in the large cab, Carrie questioned her decision to join the shopping trip. Especially when, after picking up a car seat and having it installed, Seth took the highway toward Sawyer's Bend, the large city nearest to Dover, and not the more convenient local stores. "Is there a reason we're driving thirty miles from Dover to shop?"

She'd meant the question to be teasing, but the way Seth gripped the steering wheel told her she'd hit a nerve.

"Bigger stores. Better selection."

He wasn't telling her everything. She studied him. His head was tilted to one side in a thoughtful pose, but the veins in his neck pulsed and his chin jutted slightly forward. He was upset or worried or both. Was it because of Jack? Was he regretting his commitment to the child? She wanted to ask him, but she didn't know him well enough to pry. The potential answers to her many questions left a sour taste in her mouth. Her natural skepticism was always right below the surface, but so far Seth had shown no signs of bolting. She'd wait and see how things developed.

They stopped at the mall and started their quest at one of the big anchor stores, where Seth purchased for Jack enough outfits for a month, along with expensive new shoes, and treated him to a few new toys. They even managed to get him a haircut. Carrie couldn't help but marvel at the adorable transformation in the boy. Instead of the bedraggled child on her porch, he looked like a beloved and pampered little prince.

Shopping had given them all an appetite, so they'd settled into the food court, where Jack was munching on chicken nuggets with vigor. She looked at Seth and saw him glance over his shoulder. Her curiosity grew. He'd done that multiple times, looking around, scanning the shoppers as if watching for someone he knew or perhaps wanted to avoid? She felt certain it was because Jack was with them. Was he ashamed? Or simply not ready to accept the truth? That notion didn't mesh with the way he'd enjoyed buying things for Jack.

Maybe he was worried about seeing someone he knew. It would prove awkward when he had to explain Jack. After all, Seth had been blindsided by the news he was a father. She shouldn't expect him to suddenly shout to the world he had a five-year-old child. But that's what she wanted him to do.

When they started the drive back to Dover, Carrie took a moment to assess her companion. Jack had fallen asleep the moment he was buckled into his car seat. She needed to understand for her own peace of mind. After all, Seth had told her she had a stake in Jack's well-being.

"Is something bothering you? Is it Jack?"

He glanced out the window before responding.

"Not exactly." He shook his head. "I'm not proud of that time in my life. I went to Las Vegas to experience all the things I'd been told were bad for me. I felt like I'd been set free to finally live my life the way I wanted. I found out the hard way that kind of life isn't living at all. When I came to my senses, I crawled back home and went to work for the family business. The thing is, my mom never knew anything about that year. Dad told her I was out West working on a job. She'd be so disappointed in me. And now I not only have to tell her about my past, but that she might have another grandchild."

"Are you afraid she'll reject him?"

"No, not at all. I just don't want to break her heart. She's been through a lot since my dad died. Mostly I don't want her embarrassed by my behavior. I've worked hard to clean up my reputation, but this could tarnish everything. Her life, mine and Jack's. I never realized how our thoughtless actions can come back to bite you. I thought I'd buried that whole episode."

Carrie knew only too well how the actions of the past lurked in the back of your mind like a ticking time bomb waiting for the right trigger to explode. No matter how hard you tried, you couldn't defuse it. "What are you going to do?"

"First, I have to face my mom. I'm going to see her later today. After that, I'll try to track down Tiff and get some answers and some proof. If necessary, I'll hire a private investigator, but I've got a lot of resources at my disposal I can tap into first."

"Like what?"

He grinned. "The entire law-enforcement database of the Dover Police Department. I'll be officially on duty Monday, so I'll have access to a dozen ways to track down people and information."

All the blood rushed from her head. Her stomach clenched. "You're a cop?"

"You're looking at Dover's newest police officer. I have a shiny new badge to prove it. I thought you knew."

She shook her head, unable to find her voice.

"That's where I've been the last year. After dad died, I realized it was time I followed my own dream and not his. I attended the Houston Police Academy, but it didn't take long to realize I wasn't cut out to be a big-city cop, so I came home and took a job with the Dover PD."

A cop. How had she not known? She'd only seen him from a distance a few times. Never in uniform. They both worked days, and she usually got home late and huddled inside her house until morning. They had only spoken that one time when he'd changed her tire, and their professions had never entered the conversation.

Old memories sent a shiver along her spine. Cops weren't to be trusted. Cops took away the people you cared about. Cops were incapable of compassion. Logically she knew that wasn't true, but emotionally she couldn't shake the past. Making friends with a cop was dangerous. Her greatest fear was for the truth to come out and ruin the life she'd worked so hard to create.

Her past was locked away in a courthouse file, protected from everyone. The only people who could uncover her shame were a judge and the police. A police officer like Seth.

"I don't suppose you'd consider coming with me when I talk to my mom? Just to watch Jack while I break the news. I could use the moral support."

The tension inside her chest cut off her air. "No. I don't think so. Please take me home." He jerked his head in her direction, but she kept her face angled toward the window.

"You okay?" he asked.

The tender tone of his voice scraped across her raw nerves. "Fine." She leaned against the door the rest of the way home, keenly aware of the concerned glances Seth sent her way. She had to hold it together until she got home. The moment the truck stopped in front of her house, she opened the door to bolt.

"Carrie, wait! What's going on?"

"Nothing. Tell Jack goodbye." She jogged into her house, locking the door behind her. Scraping her fingers across her scalp, she tried to make sense of what had just happened.

There was only one way to proceed. Stay clear of Seth and put an end to her involvement with Jack. She had too much at stake to risk her past being revealed now. Becoming involved in the life of a police officer was playing with fire.

She covered her face with her hands as tears formed. Would she ever be able to break free from her past?

* * *

Seth's pulse raced as he brought the truck to a stop in front of the small cottage a short distance from the large mansion that had been his family's home for three generations. His older brother and his wife and family occupied the main house now. Mom had chosen to move into the small cottage nearby.

Today he'd have to face his rebellious youth and cause his mother pain that she didn't deserve. He glanced in the rearview mirror, relieved to see Jack looking back at him, his big eyes full of curiosity.

"Where's Carrie?"

"I took her home while you were asleep. She said to tell you goodbye." Seth got out of the truck and went around to unfasten Jack from the carseat. "We're going to meet my mom. You're going to like her."

He lifted the boy from the seat, holding him snug against his chest as he walked toward the cottage. His muscles tensed as he made his way up onto the porch and tapped on the front door before entering. His mom came toward him from the kitchen, her eyes filled with concern and worry that pulled his chest even tighter. Her expression grew curious as she looked at Jack.

"Seth, honey, are you all right? You sounded so serious on the phone."

He set Jack down, keeping hold of his little hand, feeling like he was twelve again and having to explain why he'd used her Waterford crystal bowl to hold his red wiggler worms so he could go fishing. "I'm fine. I just need to talk to you and introduce you to Jack." He took a deep breath. "I think he's my son. I wanted you to know as soon as possible. I didn't want a bunch of rumors and half-truths flying around town."

His heart pounded fiercely in his chest as he watched the surprise and puzzlement move his mother's gentle features. His mom blinked, then her features softened as she looked at Jack.

"Hello, Jack."

"Hi."

"I'm glad to meet you. Do you like cupcakes?"

Jack nodded happily.

"I thought so. I just happen to have a newly iced batch in my kitchen. Why don't you show me which one you'd like to eat." She held out her hand and Jack took it without hesitation.

Some of Seth's anxiety eased. His mom had taken the news with her usual calm manner and managed to win Jack over, too. But the hard part was still to come. The explanation.

In the kitchen, his mom settled Jack at the table with two colorful, sprinkle-covered cupcakes and a glass of milk, then took a seat beside him at the counter waiting for him to begin.

"Mom, something happened last night that I need to tell you about before you hear it someplace else." Quickly he explained about Jack being left on Carrie's porch and the note naming him as Jack's father. He could read the disappointment in her blue eyes and knew what she was assuming. "It's not what you think."

He searched for the right words, unable to find them. He stood and paced off a few steps. "Do you remember that year after college when Dad and I fought all the time?"

"Yes, and you went to work out in Vegas for a while. Only you were really out there sowing some wild oats."

Seth stared in surprise. "You knew about that? Dad said he didn't want you to know."

"I knew. I spent a whole year praying for you to come to your senses and return home unharmed."

Seth sank back onto the stool. There was still more to confess. "What you don't know is that I got married."

"Only briefly."

"You knew about that, too?"

"Do you think the boy is yours?"

"Maybe. Probably, but I need to know for sure."

"I agree. You should get in touch with our attorney, Blake Prescott, and find out what steps you need to take."

"I can do better than that. I'll be officially on duty Monday, which means I can use the police databases to track his mom down."

His mother looked at Jack, happily munching on his cupcake, his little face bearing the evidence of his enjoyment. "He looks exactly like you at that age. He has your eyes and your smile."

"I know." He nodded, not sure if her assessment made him feel better or worse. The circumstantial evidence was mounting, but he needed facts. "What if it turns out he's not mine? I'm already feeling attached. I don't know if I could let him go."

His mother squeezed his hand. "For now let's assume he is. You do whatever you must to get to the truth. We'll place this in the Lord's hands and see how it works out. What are your plans for him while you're at work?"

"I don't know yet." He raised his hand to forestall her next statement. "No. You're not going to babysit. You already have your hands full with Linc's new baby and filling in for the other grandkids. I'll work something out. This is my problem."

He thought he saw a flicker of pride lighten her eyes. "Well, you could enroll him in the church preschool. They also provide after-school care. I'm sure Kathy could make room for one more little fellow."

"I'll look into it."

"What do you plan on telling people? You can't show up with a child without some kind of explanation."

"I don't know. I haven't thought that far ahead. I don't even know how I'll tell the rest of the family."

She placed her hand on his cheek and smiled. "You bring Jack for Sunday dinner tomorrow. We'll tell them then and decide as a family how to proceed."

"Is it okay if I bring Carrie? She might have some insight into how to handle things."

"Carrie? The neighbor who found Jack?"

"Carrie Fletcher. She's been a trouper. I wouldn't have known what to do if it hadn't been for her. She has a real passion for kids like Jack."

"I know her. She's the new head of special events at the church. From everything I've heard, she's doing a wonderful job."

"I think she said something about working at Peace

Community. We've mainly talked about Jack." He wiped a hand across his mouth. "I doubt she'll come."

"What happened?"

"She found out I was a cop and her reaction was puzzling. She shut down and hardly said a word the rest of the way home. When I stopped at her house, she ran inside like the bogeyman was after her."

"Maybe she's wary because of the danger involved in your line of work. That's the main reason your father was always against you going into law enforcement."

"I know." He knew how the danger associated with the job could tear apart a policeman's family life. His uncle had been a cop killed in the line of duty.

Seth wanted to believe his mother was right, but something about Carrie's reaction ate at him. He usually received two responses when people learned he was a cop. They were either curious about the job or puzzled at why he'd chosen a dangerous profession. Carrie's reaction had been more like... Seth swallowed around the lump in his throat. Like someone who was trying to hide something. He'd seen that look on the faces of people he'd arrested. That look of being cornered with no way out.

That didn't make sense. What would Carrie have to hide? Perhaps it had something to do with her childhood. Her comments and her attitude suggested she might have more in common with Jack than he realized.

He didn't want her to be uncomfortable around him. On the contrary, he wanted to get to know her better. And Jack was the link. At the very least he wanted to reassure her she had nothing to fear from him. He'd give her some time to adjust to the idea of his job. He felt sure he could ease her concerns. After all, being a cop in Dover wasn't anything like being a cop in Houston. Here, he could focus on serving and protecting the people in his community and not the endless stream of senseless violence that had dragged him down.

Monday morning dawned bright and sunny with temperatures promised in the midseventies. Carrie dressed in a new pair of linen pants and a long peach top, plus some dangling silver earrings. The outfit lifted her spirits, and she arrived at the church eager to tackle her hectic work schedule. It was exactly what she needed to put the weekend behind her. Learning that Seth was a police officer had left her battling old fears and memories.

She had called her friend and mentor, Mavis Tanner, for some advice. Mavis had been her first and biggest blessing from the Lord. She'd taken Carrie under her wing, introduced her to the Lord, and helped her get her GED and enroll in community college. Without Mavis, Carrie would be living a very different life.

Her friend had gently reminded her that her concerns about Seth were nothing more than her old insecurities bubbling to the surface. Then she pointed out that the Lord had forgiven her and the past couldn't hurt her unless she allowed it. She'd felt better after their talk, but she hadn't told Mavis about her attraction to Seth. She had to sort that out on her own.

She wondered what Seth had done with Jack today. It was his first official day on the job. He'd called her a couple times, but she'd ignored him. She needed more time to absorb the fact that he was a police officer. Her mind and her heart had battled all night. But now she needed to concentrate on her work. There was a mountain of arrangements to make for the upcoming picnic celebration. She had no time to waste on her neighbor.

Thankfully, the day passed quickly. The only thing left on her schedule was the meeting this evening with the committee heads for the anniversary picnic. She had one volunteer spot to fill and several adjustments to the activities to discuss, but nothing major. The plans were all coming together nicely.

After a quick bite to eat in her office, she made her way to the meeting room. Kathy met her coming from the opposite direction. "You look frazzled. Everything okay? I didn't have a chance to talk to you at church yesterday."

"I spent the time between services fielding questions about the picnic. I have to admit it'll be a relief when it's all over."

"I keep telling you that you need an assistant."

Carrie arched her eyebrows. "Like Ralph?"

Kathy rolled her eyes. "No. Like Ralph *used* to be."

The committee members filed in and Carrie started the meeting by going over the positions still needing to be filled. Midway through, Seth Montgomery slipped in and took a seat at the back of the room. Her throat went dry. He was dressed in full uniform. The white shirt with its military-style tabs and pockets contrasted sharply with his olive-toned skin and made his shoulders appear even broader. He was a handsome man, a man who carried himself with confidence and authority. A man with the power to uncover her deepest secret.

Thankfully, the meeting came to a close quickly, and she hoped Seth would leave with the others. Unfortunately, no one had stepped up to be her gofer. It was just as well. The extra work would keep her too busy to think about Seth or Jack.

"Carrie, guess what I found for you?"

She glanced up to see Kathy approaching the table, followed by a smiling Seth Montgomery. She tried to hide her discomfort behind a stiff smile and avoid eye contact. The uniform stirred old anxieties, but she couldn't deny it also added a layer of masculinity to his already compelling appeal. No doubt, he'd dismissed her as a basket case, given the way she'd bolted from his truck the other day. It didn't matter since she'd be keeping her distance from now on.

Kathy spread her arms. "Meet your new anniversary-picnic assistant."

Seth flashed his white teeth and rested his hands on his duty belt. "Kathy told me you needed help, so I decided to step up."

He couldn't be serious. "You have a full-time job. You won't have time to do all the small errands I'll need help with." Not to mention she was trying to avoid Seth, not work side by side with him.

"Are you turning me down?"

She searched for a polite response. "No. But you said yourself you're starting your new job, and then there's Jack to take care of. I need someone flexible who can act as a gofer. The way Ralph used to."

"And that's the beauty of my job, Carrie. After this next week, I'll be on the midday shift. Noon to eight. That leaves all morning to run errands." He held up a finger. "Plus, who better to be your gofer than a police officer? I'm on the road all day, I have access everywhere in town and it'll give me plenty of opportunity to interact with the community. Part of my job is being visible around town and building goodwill between the department and the citizens. I already ran it by Captain Durrant and he's on board."

Carrie's hopes faded. She really needed help to get all the details of the picnic together, but not with Seth. "And Jack? Who's going to take care of him while you're running my errands?"

"I enrolled him in the preschool here this morning. I tried to let you know, but you weren't answering your phone."

Backed into a corner, she frantically tried to think of other reasons to refuse his offer. He leaned forward and she caught a hint of his spicy aftershave and a whiff of leather. His nearness stole the starch from her knees, forcing her to grasp the table for support. She could not develop any attraction for her neighbor—a man with the ability to destroy her life.

"Carrie, I owe you big-time for helping out with Jack. This is my way of paying you back. It'll work out. It's a win-win for both of us. I'll help you with the picnic, and maybe you could help by watching Jack from time to time. He misses you. He keeps looking for you."

Now he was being unfair, using Jack to get to her.

"I appreciate what you're trying to do, but this position has always been Ralph's job."

Seth grinned and tugged on his earlobe. "Ralph is getting older and can barely find his way to church."

She bristled. "He's a dear man who has devoted himself to this church. I wouldn't dream of breaking his heart."

"What's this about you replacing me?"

They turned around to see Ralph shuffling toward them, his shoulders bent forward, his dark eyes snapping from under the brim of his Mississippi Braves ball cap.

Carrie exhaled a heavy sigh. This is what she'd dreaded. "No, Ralph, you haven't been replaced."

The old man muttered a soft curse and tugged at his cap. "Better not. No one's putting me out to pasture."

Seth stepped toward him and extended his hand. "Hello, Mr. Ralph. Remember me? Seth Montgomery."

Ralph ignored the hand, pointing a finger at him, instead. "You're the rapscallion who threw all my hay out of the barn loft onto the floor so you and your hoodlum friends could jump into it."

"Yes, sir. That was me." He gestured toward his uniform. "But I've rejected those ways and embraced the law."

Ralph harrumphed. "You the one trying to take my job?"

"No, sir. Never. But I'd like to be your apprentice, learn the ropes from the master, so to speak."

Carrie watched the anger fade from the old man's dark eyes and the shoulders straighten. "Fine by me, but you'd better stay on your toes. This ain't a job for slackers." Ralph wagged a finger at them as he walked away.

Carrie dared a look at Seth. "Thank you. That was very sweet. You preserved his pride." Seth unleashed his smile in her direction and her insides wobbled.

"So, does that earn me the position? I promise I'll keep him in the loop. I like the old guy."

Carrie knew she'd regret it, but she really had no choice. Mavis was right. She had to stop worrying. Seth was only trying to help. "Fine. But I warn you, you'll hear from me a lot between now and the picnic. Especially those last few weeks."

Seth grinned and held out his hand. "Deal. And it's even better that we live next door. We're a good team, Carrie. We can work together on the picnic and help Jack."

She took his hand. It was warm and strong and filled her with a sense of security. Seth would always make those he cared about feel secure. Being protective was in his nature. She'd seen that firsthand in the way he'd stepped up to take care of Jack. He would make a great father and a devoted husband, when the time came.

And he would choose a woman of strong character from a good family. Not someone like her. A thief with a criminal record.

Chapter Four

Seth scanned the area around the municipal complex as his temporary partner, Phil Hagen, pulled the cruiser out of the police-station lot and onto the highway. Traffic was heavy with residents heading to work. Farther up the road, yellow school buses lumbered into the sprawling attendance center of the Dover school system. He kept his gaze moving, looking for anything unusual or out of place. Major crimes in Dover were few. Most of their calls were for accidents, DUIs and domestic disputes. There hadn't been a murder in town in years. Even so, Phil had assured him there was still enough criminal behavior to keep the Dover PD busy.

Today they were patrolling the southern section of the town, where a series of burglaries had recently been reported. Neighborhoods there ran the gamut from lower-income wooden homes and the only apartment complex in town to the newly constructed subdivisions of large homes that were mainly owned by people from Sawyer's Bend looking for a quieter lifestyle.

"So what's the opinion on these thefts?"

"The captain thinks it's a bunch of bored teenagers breaking into homes, taking game consoles and tablets just for the thrill of it. It's only the homes in the new subdivision that are being hit."

"Sounds like they could use something to occupy their time. Maybe I can get Kent Blackburn, the youth pastor from the church, to look into it. He could get them to come to the group on Sunday nights or join a Bible study."

Phil shook his head. "Yeah, right. Church is the answer to everything, isn't it?"

"It should be. Teens are searching for their identity and they don't always look in the right places. Kent has a real way with teenagers. They trust him."

Phil merely shook his head and fell silent. Seth returned his focus to the things happening outside the car window, but his inner focus was on Jack and Carrie. He hadn't talked to her since she'd agreed reluctantly to accept him as her assistant. He wasn't sure if she was avoiding him or simply busy. He'd stopped by her office the last two days after he dropped Jack off at preschool, but it was always empty, and when he inquired he was told the same thing by everyone. "She's around here somewhere." If nothing else he'd learned that she was extremely committed to her job.

Jack, on the other hand, had seen Carrie every day. He spent the ride home each afternoon talking about school and how Carrie came and visited him at lunch or during recess. While he was glad she was looking in on the boy, he didn't like the idea that she might be avoiding him. He had a plan to address the situation this evening. He only hoped it worked.

A car blew through the stop sign, and Phil hit the lights and pursued the blue sedan, which slowed and pulled over. A ticket was issued and they continued their patrol. The morning passed quickly with a response to a woman who had found a gun buried in the spot where she was putting a new flower bed, and the apprehension of a man trying to steal a car out near the county-line road.

Their lunch break was interrupted by a call to go to see a contractor in the old Victorian section of town who had reported stolen materials from the job site.

Seth sensed Phil glancing in his direction. "What?"

"So you going to tell me about this kid that popped up in your life or is there some reason you want to keep him a big secret?"

Seth glanced out the window and searched for the right words. He knew the man would want to know and he was surprised that it had taken this long for him to ask. Phil wasn't shy about butting into other people's business. The family had decided to simply explain that Jack had been with his mother and now he was with Seth. No other explanation would be given until the whole truth was known. "Jack has been with his mother, and now he's come to stay with me." It was the truth, but not the whole truth, and he didn't like the feeling it left in his chest.

"So you have a kid, huh? That's rich. Guess your love-'em-and-leave-'em past finally caught up with you, huh?"

Seth set his jaw. Phil had never been a close friend, merely one of the guys he'd hung around with growing up, and since being temporarily partnered with him for his first week on the job, he'd been reacquainted with the man's lack of tact and understanding. "Jack's mother and I were married."

"Do tell? Rumor around town says you didn't know you had a kid."

His fingers curled into a fist on his thigh. This is what he'd feared—rumors and gossip that would embarrass his family and, especially, Jack. "Don't believe everything you hear, Phil."

A low chuckle filled the car. "No, that might tarnish the mighty Montgomery name, now, wouldn't it? We can't have that."

"Just what do you have against my family? You've had a chip on your shoulder all your life."

"Nothing. I just get sick of hearing how superior y'all are. Big house, big company, running everything in town. It's a wonder none of your clan has run for mayor, then you could really take over."

Seth let the dig slide. He was in no mood to spar with Phil. What he wanted was to talk to Carrie. He had questions about Jack, things that had happened in the last few days he needed to tell her about. Besides, Jack missed her. He kept going to the window, looking for her and Leo.

As soon as his shift was over he was going to pick up Jack, swing by Angelo's and get a large pizza. Then he'd show up at her door. She wasn't going to avoid him forever.

* * *

There were still a few minutes of daylight left in the sky when Carrie got home, a perfect opportunity to take her glass of sweet tea onto the front porch and enjoy the explosion of spring. The azaleas were in full bloom along the side of her house and in the park across the street. Pink, white, red, coral and purple flowers, all mixed together like an exquisite Monet painting. The confederate jasmine that climbed up the side of her porch and made a nice privacy screen was blooming and filling the air with its sweet, heady fragrance.

She'd had a very productive day at work, though none of it had revolved around the anniversary picnic. Her regular duties took a lot of time. The picnic was an extra project. She should have called Seth for help with a few things but hadn't. She wanted to avoid that situation for as long as possible. It was a futile hope. Especially since she took time out of each day to check on Jack in the preschool in the morning and during after-school care in the afternoon. The little guy was always so glad to see her, and the toothy grin he gave her turned her insides to soft goo. His sweet hugs unleashed a nurturing part of her nature she was beginning to enjoy.

Each night she longed to talk to Seth to see how they were doing and ask how Jack was adjusting. She'd talked herself out of it each time, though, try as she might, she just couldn't keep thoughts of the pair from invading her mind. She couldn't decide which little-boy smile touched her more—Jack's innocent, uninhibited grin or Seth's slow one, which brought a knowing twinkle to the corner of his eyes.

"Miss Carrie."

"Jack!" Jerked from her thoughts, her tea sloshed over the rim of her glass. She set it down and waved, smiling as the little boy raced across the lawn and up onto her porch. He launched himself into her arms.

"We have pizza for you!"

Carrie glanced up as Seth strolled onto her sidewalk and stopped at the bottom of her porch steps. In his hands, he held a large pizza box that smelled wonderful and drew a rumble from her stomach.

"We're inviting ourselves to supper. Hope you don't mind."

The teasing grin on his face made his dark eyes twinkle, and the dimples beside his mouth made her heart flutter unexpectedly. How was a woman supposed to refuse the sweet hugs of a five-year-old and the very appealing smile of a handsome man?

"Not at all. That's very nice of you. I love pizza."

Leo greeted them at the door as they entered, and Jack squatted down to pet him. Carrie made her way to the kitchen, the aroma of hot pizza filling the air. "Do I smell green peppers and onions?"

Seth placed the box on the table. "Is that okay? I take mine with everything on it. Except mushrooms."

"Me, too."

Seth grinned. "Interesting. Another thing we have in common."

Not so great. Still, it was interesting that they liked the same toppings. After they ate the pizza and the kitchen was cleaned up, they went to the living room where Jack and Leo were playing.

Seth sat beside her on the sofa. "I have to confess the pizza was only part of the reason we came over. I wanted to catch you up on what's happening with Jack, and to find out why you've been avoiding us."

How could she explain that she missed seeing them, but that her irrational fears kept her hostage? "I'm just busy, and when I get home I usually hibernate."

Seth nodded, his expression revealing his skepticism. "Right. Well, I know that you've been checking on Jack at preschool every day this week. He tells me all about it when he gets home. He also keeps asking why we can't visit you and why you don't come over. I didn't know what to tell him."

She shrugged. "I didn't want to intrude. How's Jack doing?"

"Still sleeping with me. He starts out in his own room, but by the middle of the night, he's climbing into my bed. I don't mind. He doesn't take up much space."

The tender smile on his lips put a warm light in his deep blue eyes, and she found it hard to look away. He really did care for Jack. "He feels safe with you." Jack turned his attention to his car and Leo scurried to her feet.

Seth tilted his head. "But you don't. Is that why you've been avoiding me? Does this have anything to do with me being a cop? You seemed upset when you found out. Is it because of the risk involved with the job?"

Carrie looked away, lifting Leo into her lap as she prepared her response. She'd hoped he'd forgotten about that. Refusing to explain would only raise more questions. Maybe a partial answer would satisfy him.

"No. It's not the job exactly. I grew up in a rough neighborhood. Mom died when I was young and it was only me and my brother after my dad walked out, and to us, policemen were the enemy. They weren't to be trusted. I knew they were supposed to be there to help, but when they showed up, it always ended up with friends and neighbors being taken away, or innocent people being hurt. I've always avoided the police, so finding out you were one of them was a shock."

"I can understand that. I'm sorry you grew up with that kind of opinion. I hope I can show you that we really are the good guys. We're here to help. You can't blame us all for the few bad apples."

"I know."

"Good. I want us to be friends. After all, we're Jack's surrogate parents in a way. I need your input with him. I'm new at this dad thing and I have a lot of questions. I want to do things right with him."

"You can always ask your mom. How did that go, by the way?" She hoped she could distract him with other topics.

He leaned forward, resting his arms on his thighs. "Better than I expected. She took to Jack as if he was part of the family already. No questions asked. And it turns out she knew about my time in Vegas, after all. She said she'd prayed for me every day. Her prayers probably saved my life."

"And now you're saving Jack's."

Seth shook his head and glanced at the little boy.

"I don't know about that. I'm just trying to get to the truth." He looked at her and smiled. "And the truth is, I'm supposed to be your assistant for the big picnic, and yet you haven't called me for help once."

She shrugged. "That's because I'm still finalizing the details. Don't worry. You'll get plenty of calls from me in the coming weeks."

"Tell me about your idea. What do you have planned?"

The topic was one she loved to talk about. "I want this to be like an old-fashioned event with sack races and croquet, and I was thinking about pony rides."

"No kidding? Then I'm your man. Amos Jefferson keeps ponies. He used to bring them to local fairs and other events. He had the whole getup—the sweep, the carousel with a striped canopy. He stopped a few years ago. I'm sure I could get him to come out of retirement for the picnic. Consider it done."

"Thanks. That was easy."

Seth spread his hands in an it's-taken-care-of gesture. "You're welcome. Now that I've helped you, maybe you can help me."

A small knot of anxiety formed in the center of her chest. What would he expect from her? "If I can."

"I start my assigned shift next week. I'll be working from noon to eight for a few months, which means I won't be able to pick Jack up from after-school care. I was hoping you'd bring him home with you, then I'll pick him up when I get off."

She desperately wanted to say no, but the thought of taking care of Jack was too exciting to pass up. She couldn't deny she'd lost her heart to the little boy. "I'd be happy to."

Seth's blue eyes filled with amusement. "See, I told you we made a great team."

Carrie couldn't look away from his twinkling blue gaze. When he looked at her like that, she felt a pull drawing her to him. He made her feel as if she was the only person in the world. It took great effort to shift her focus to more important matters. "You mentioned that you had news about Jack. Have you found his mother?"

The warm light in Seth's eyes faded into sadness. "No. All I've found is a long trail of addresses stretching across the West and ending in Missouri. Apparently, she moved whenever a new boyfriend showed up."

"That must have been hard on Jack."

"Yeah. I'm trying not to think about it. I'm searching for his birth certificate. From what I can figure out, Tiff had to have given birth in either California or Nevada according to the trail she left behind."

"Will that prove you're his father?"

"It would be a good start, but you can write anything on that certificate. That's why I'm checking under both our last names." He clasped his hands together. "I also had a DNA test taken when I took Jack to the doctor."

She grasped Seth's forearm, her pulse racing. "Is he all right? Was he sick?"

Seth laid his hand over hers, sending a warmth through her chest that made her want to smile.

"He's fine. Mom suggested I have him checked out just to make sure he was healthy. Given the way he looked the night he showed up on your porch, I thought it was a good idea. He's fine. A little underweight and in need of some vitamins, but otherwise he's in good health."

Carrie exhaled a sigh of relief. "I'm so glad. Now we can concentrate on keeping him happy."

Seth looked over at the little boy, who was stretched out on the floor with Carrie's shih tzu. "I just want him to feel safe. Every night when I put him to bed, he asks if I'm going away. I have to reassure him that I'll be there in the morning. I think he must have nightmares, and they send him running him to my room. He's scared and shaking and he plasters himself to my side. Eventually he falls asleep."

"Poor Jack. Bedtime is hard for little ones. He feels safe with you. You make everyone feel safe." Heat surged up her neck and into her cheeks. What made her say that? She tugged her hand from under his and lowered her eyes. "It's probably why you're a police officer." She dared a look at Seth. He was studying her with an expression she couldn't name. Had she said too much? Gotten too personal?

A slow smile moved over his lips and his deep blue eyes softened. "Thank you. I think that's the nicest compliment I've ever received."

Their gazes meshed and held. Seth broke the contact with a quick glance at his watch. "I'd better get our little man home and ready for bed. Tomorrow's my last day as a ride-along. I'll be on my own next week. Which makes this weekend my last free one for a while. I thought about taking Jack to the lake on Saturday. Would you like to join us?"

"I'd love to." She regretted her words the moment she blurted them out. Common sense told her to not get any closer to Seth or Jack, but she was eager to be there when Jack saw the lake for the first time.

Seth gathered up Jack's things and said goodbye, smiling as Jack gave her a big hug around her neck. She watched them from her porch as they walked home, her anticipation growing. She looked forward to going with them to the lake tomorrow and babysitting Jack. It was clear she would have to accept that her life was entangled with the Montgomery men. Maybe she was worrying for nothing. After all, Seth wouldn't be interested in someone like her. He was one of Dover's favorite sons, the member of a well-respected family. And a cop.

Back inside her house, she walked to the window, smiling when she saw Jack's little face peeking out, waving frantically. She waved back, then the child disappeared. She turned away, noticing how quiet and empty her little cottage felt. She'd always cherished her time alone, but her neighbors had changed that. Without Jack the energy level was drastically reduced. And Seth's vibrant male presence never failed to leave a lingering sense of warmth.

Leo whined and looked up at her. Was he missing the Montgomerys, too?

"Come on, Leo, let's turn in early."

Carrie strained her neck to look into the backseat of Seth's truck, smiling when her gaze landed on the little boy in the car seat. Jack had been asleep on his feet after a day at Shiloh Lake. Seth had carried him the last few yards to the truck and buckled him in. He looked so sweet and peaceful.

The large cashew-shaped lake was situated five miles north of Dover. Fishing camps hugged the eastern shore and a residential area of cabins perched on the other side. In addition to hiking, boating, camping and a picnic area, there was a small area for swimming. She caught a glimpse of a large lodge nestled under tall trees. Seth had explained that at one time Pine Tree Lodge was an active vacation spot, complete with a restaurant and space for large events. The owner had become ill and closed it down several years ago.

"I think we might have overdone it today. Maybe we should have split this adventure up into two trips."

Seth chuckled. "It wouldn't have mattered. He would have thrown himself into the day no matter what. He's five. It's what little boys do." He glanced over at her, holding her gaze a moment. "You're really good with kids, Carrie. You have a very nurturing way about you. I'm guessing you plan on having a half-dozen kids someday don't you?"

Carrie had to clear her throat before speaking. "Why would you think that?"

"I've never met anyone more suited for motherhood than you."

She knew he meant it to be a compliment, but he didn't understand her history. "No, I don't plan on getting married. I don't think it's in the cards for me."

"You're wrong. You'd be a great mother. You're wonderful with Jack."

"Thank you, but that's why I plan on devoting myself

to the children who really need me as a social worker. That doesn't leave much time for a relationship."

"No, guess not."

Seth steered the truck into the narrow alley behind their homes and pulled to a stop in his driveway. He glanced back at the still-sleeping boy. "I'll have to carry him in. I think he's out for the night."

"You get him and I'll bring his treasures inside." Jack didn't flinch as he was released from the harness and positioned in Seth's arms. Carrie grabbed his small jacket and the backpack Jack had filled with everything he'd found today. His treasures included rocks, leaves, twigs, a piece of snakeskin and several wilted flowers. She knew exactly how he felt. This adventure might be the only one he'd had and he wanted to hoard the mementos.

Carrie found Seth and Jack in the master bedroom. "You're not going to put him in his own bed?"

He shook his head. "He'll just end up here, anyway."

Seth's cell blared a loud song, and he quickly slid it from his pocket. "I've got to take this. Would you mind finishing up?"

"Sure." Getting Jack undressed and into his pj's was like dressing a wet noodle, but once he was snug under the covers, she stroked his silky hair and kissed his cheek. Seth was right—she would love to have kids of her own. But that wasn't likely to happen. The thought gave birth to a deep and painful sadness.

Seth stepped into the room. "Did he wake up?"

"No, he's worn-out."

Seth bent and kissed his son, then motioned for her

to join him. They settled in the kitchen. "Can I fix you a cup of coffee? It'll only take a minute. I have one of those pod things."

"It's late."

"I want to tell you about that phone call. It concerns the picnic."

"Oh, okay."

"That was Amos. I'm going out to his place tomorrow afternoon to work out the details of the pony ride. He's excited to be doing this again. He said he missed seeing the kid's faces when they get on those ponies for the first time. And, before you ask, I already called Ralph and told him I needed his help, so he's coming along, too."

Carrie smiled at his thoughtfulness and consideration. How was she supposed to resist a guy with such a big heart? "Thank you. I really appreciate this."

He hunched his shoulders and bent forward slightly. "I was hoping you'd come along, too. I'm sure you'll have plenty of questions."

And there it was. Another chance to spend time with Seth, and another opportunity to be strong and steer clear. "I'd love to, but I need to study in the afternoon. I'm behind on my course work and I don't want to fail this class." Did she see disappointment in his dark blue eyes? Did that mean he wanted to spend time with her, or was he only looking for help with Jack?

"I understand. I'll let you know how it goes. That's what an assistant does, right?"

His smile was nearly her undoing. "Right. In fact we need to get together and go over my plan for the picnic.

There's a lot to coordinate and you might be able to take on a few other things to help out."

"Great. I'll pick up another pizza."

"How about I cook this time?"

"It'll have to be a late supper. Remember I won't get off until eight."

"No problem. I'll feed Jack, then you and I can eat while we go over the picnic schedule."

"Sounds like a plan."

Carrie said goodbye and hurried across the lawn toward her house. Had she just arranged a date with Seth? She had a degree to earn, a job to manage and a huge project to complete. How had one little five-year-old boy shifted all her priorities? Or was it the boy's father that had her so unsettled?

Either way it was time to start growing that thicker skin. But how did she disengage her emotions? Seth already looked upon the child as his son, but all he had to go on was that scribbled note. If it proved to be a lie, Seth would be crushed. Even she wanted the pair to be related. However, there was nothing she could do to about that. All she could really do for them was to pray that Seth would find positive proof that Jack was his son. She didn't want to think about the alternative.

Seth parked the cruiser near the Peace Community Church office Tuesday afternoon and killed the engine. He leaned back in the driver's seat, staring straight ahead, wondering again why he'd come here. He could have gone to his mom's or to see one of his brothers. For some reason the only person he wanted to talk to was Carrie. She was his partner when it came to Jack. She needed to know what he'd learned this morning.

His feet felt like lead as he took the few steps up to the back door. Carrie's office was the third one down the hall. As he passed the first doorway, a woman stepped out. Lorna Gathers, a longtime church member and his former high school English teacher, greeted him with a frown.

"I hear you have a new family member."

Seth froze, striving to keep a neutral expression on his face. "Miss Gathers. How are you today?"

She arched her eyebrows. "Interesting, isn't it, how our past sins always catch up with us?" She pivoted and walked off, calling over her shoulder as she went. "I expected better from you, Seth Montgomery. Your mother must be crushed."

Seth's insides burned. This was what he'd feared, the backlash from some of the so-called good people of Dover. Thankfully, most had been circumspect about Jack. But there were always those who felt it was their place to point out his failings.

Carrie's door was open and he stopped at the threshold, watching her work. The sight of her chased away the lingering irritation from Miss Gathers's comment. His pretty neighbor was intent on her task, her sweet mouth pulled to one side as she concentrated. The light green top she wore brought out the pink in her cheeks. Her fingers absently tugged at her hair, making him smile. He could watch her all day. She was a fascinating woman, and adorable, too. A dangerous combination.

He tapped on the door frame, and she glanced up

as he stepped into the room. She smiled and his heart flipped. He knew he'd made the right decision to come here.

"Hey."

"Seth. What are you doing here?" Her expression shifted to one of concern. "Everything okay?"

He nodded. "Fine. I, uh, can you take a break for a few minutes? I need to talk to you."

A flash of alarm darted through her eyes, then quickly vanished. "Yes, of course. Why don't we go to the prayer garden? We'll have privacy there and it's a nice day to be outside."

The small garden behind the sanctuary was bursting with flowering azaleas and fat blooms of lavender wisteria, filling the air with their sweet perfume. Carrie chose a wooden bench near the back corner behind the fountain, and Seth wasted no time in getting to the point.

"I got this in the mail today." He pulled an envelope from his shirt pocket and handed it to her. Her forehead creased as she read the return address.

"What is this?"

"Open it." His heart pounded hard inside his rib cage. He wasn't sure what he expected Carrie to do. He simply wanted her to know. And maybe offer some comfort and encouragement to him the way she always did for Jack.

"It's Jack's birth certificate. This is good news, isn't it? It proves he's yours?"

"Look at the line for parents' names."

She read from the document, "'Mother—Paula Ann

Schulman. Father—Unknown.' Oh, Seth. What does this mean?"

"Paula was Tiff's real name. She changed it to Tiffany Lane when she went to Vegas." He ran a hand along the side of his neck. "It means either she really didn't know who the father was or she was trying to keep the truth from me."

The look of sympathy in her blue eyes wrapped around him, chasing away the sharp edges of his disappointment. When she reached out and grasped his forearm with her small hand, the warmth of her touch spread through him like a warm summer breeze.

"I'm sorry. I was hoping this would be the answer you needed."

He took her hand in his, gently squeezing her fingers. Odd, how such a tiny hand could hold such soothing power. "Me, too. Now I'll have to wait on the DNA results."

"When is that due?"

"Not for a few more weeks. In the meantime I'll keep trying to find Tiff." He looked into her sky blue eyes and realized he didn't want to break the contact. Carrie abruptly looked away and tugged her hand from his.

"Any progress tracking her down?"

He inhaled a deep breath and shifted his position slightly, though it did nothing to diminish his acute awareness of her softness or her beauty, which rivaled the flowering shrubs behind her. He rubbed his forehead. When had he become a romantic? "The last place she was seen was Branson, Missouri. No clue as to where she went after that."

"She moves around a lot. Does she have a job that requires a lot of travel?"

Seth straightened. How would Carrie react to the truth about his former wife? "I think there's something I should tell you about Tiff. When I met her, she was dancing in the chorus of a Vegas show. To a small-town guy like me, she was exotic, wild and very exciting. We married in haste. It didn't take long to realize we'd made a mistake. Rather, she realized it. I'd been throwing money around. She thought I was rich and could provide her with material things. The relationship deteriorated after she lost her job and I couldn't support us. She didn't even wait for the divorce papers to be drawn up before she found someone else."

It was all so clear to him now, but at the time he'd been captivated by her beauty and the attention she'd lavished on him—as long as the presents kept coming and the fun never ended. "She was always chasing the next rainbow, looking for the pot of gold."

"I'm sorry. I know how easy it is to be lured in by someone attractive and attentive."

He doubted that, but it was sweet of her to say so. "I'd like to think it was the only time, but it seems to be a habit of mine—picking unsuitable women. That's not the worst of it. I found out she was working with a friend in an insurance-fraud scheme. She'd been arrested multiple times. I can really pick 'em, huh?"

He met Carrie's gaze and his heart jerked. The look of shock in her blue eyes condemned his shameful behavior. He'd said too much. Whatever good opinion of him she might have had was destroyed. He looked away. It had been a dumb idea to come talk to her.

"You couldn't have known."

"But I should have. I've learned my lesson. I'll be more aware next time. Especially now that I might have Jack to consider. I'll take my time, make sure we have the same interests and values. I want a partner in life, a forever kind of woman." Great. He'd practically told her he was interested. *Smooth move, Montgomery.* "Not that I'm in any hurry to get involved with anyone." He stood, rubbing his palms together, feeling like an awkward teenager. "Sorry to dump this on you."

Carrie rose, a faint smile on her lips. "I'm glad you did. I want to know how things are going with Jack. We're in this together, remember?"

"I do, and I can't tell you how much that means to me. Thanks. I'll see you after work."

He walked out of the small garden, keenly aware of her gaze on his back. Why had he spilled his guts to her like that? He never talked about his life in Vegas, and he'd *never* told anyone about Tiff's involvement with the fraud ring. He'd buried it deep in the back of his mind. But Jack had opened up that vault of shame, and now he was having to look at things from a different perspective. Miss Gathers was right. His sins had caught up with him, and now all of Dover would know.

Chapter Five

Carrie took her time going back to the office, her emotions twisting like taffy on a stretching machine. She'd been so excited to see the birth certificate only to have her hopes dashed when it had proved useless. The disappointment in Seth's eyes had wrenched her heart. He'd looked like a little boy who'd lost his beloved pet. She wanted to put her arms around him and give him a hug, the way she did with Jack. But her sympathy had been supplanted quickly by shock and horror. Seth's former wife was a criminal.

She fought to keep her expression from revealing her alarm, hoping he wouldn't see the truth in her eyes. Learning about Seth's ex-wife had only pointed out why she needed to keep her emotions under control. He'd already been betrayed by a woman with a criminal history. If he ever found out about Carrie's past, he would walk away without a second thought.

Her heart weighed heavy inside her chest as she made her way down the hallway. Her attraction to Seth was stronger than she'd thought possible. She never allowed herself to even notice most men. Her one brief relationship had lasted long enough for her to realize that he only wanted to conquer her, to control her. She'd walked away in time, but it had served to reinforce her belief that she was a horrible judge of men, and a romantic relationship wasn't in her future.

Then Seth Montgomery had changed her tire—and changed her mind with a simple, kind gesture.

What she didn't know was how she was going to keep her feelings in check and still see him and Jack. The picnic organization would be ramping up in the next few weeks, and she would need Seth's help.

Back in her office, she started checking emails. Not surprisingly, a problem had developed with one of her orders. She'd learned quickly that part of her job involved constantly putting out fires. She clicked on the email from Party Time Events. They were claiming they'd lost her order for the two bouncy houses for the anniversary picnic. This was one thing she didn't want messed up. The children were already looking forward to them. It took only a moment to pull up the confirmation from the folder and send it back. Just to be sure, she picked up the phone and placed a call to the company.

Her mood lightened. This was what she enjoyed and what she excelled at—problem solving, organizing and bringing things together.

If only she could do the same for Seth and Jack. But there was little she could do to solve their problem except continue to pray for a good outcome. She'd have to leave that in the Lord's hands.

* * *

Seth stood inside the master bedroom later that night watching his son sleep. His son. He hadn't realized how much he'd believed that until the birth certificate had arrived. Why had Tiff left the name of the father off the document? Had she been trying to get back at him, or was she really unsure who had fathered her child?

And if he wasn't Jack's father, who was? And would he come for him someday? The idea of losing Jack to someone else, or being forced to turn him over to the foster-care system knotted his stomach. He couldn't lose his son. The cobalt eyes, the instant recognition by Seth's mother, the little gestures and quirks that were so much like his own proved that Jack was his. He believed that to his core.

But the legal system wouldn't take his word for it. Now he was forced to wait for the DNA results. The thought weighed heavy on his mind. The longer Jack was with him the harder it would be to let him go. Never in his wildest dreams would he have imagined the intense emotion that had been born when Jack arrived in his life. The love he felt for the little boy was stronger and ran deeper than he'd ever thought possible. His need to protect him bordered on fierce, and when Jack smiled at him his heart melted, his insides softened, and he wanted to show him the wonders of life. He was already thinking about signing him up for a baseball team.

Seth shook off the nonsensical thoughts. He should be concentrating on his job, getting familiar with the Dover PD system, but Jack kept him distracted. Not a good idea for a cop on duty. When he wasn't thinking about Jack, he was thinking about Carrie. Funny, he couldn't separate the two.

Quietly he made his way out of the room. He'd been restless and unable to sleep. Fearful of waking Jack, he'd gotten up to go watch mindless television for a while, hoping to distract his troubled mind.

He glanced out the window as he entered the living room, surprised to see every light in Carrie's cottage blazing. It was nearly one thirty in the morning. Was she still awake? He pulled the curtain aside and took a closer look. Perhaps she was studying. He knew some of the responsibility for Jack had no doubt cut into her quiet time. He knew her classes were important, so she was probably pulling an all-nighter to catch up.

Letting the curtain fall back into place, he stretched out on the sofa and picked up the remote. It wasn't the first time he'd noticed her lights on until late, but he hadn't thought much about it. She'd simply been the cute neighbor and he'd assumed she worked odd hours. Now that they were friends, he wondered if she was a night owl or maybe had trouble sleeping. Still, it was odd that every light in the house was lit.

He considered calling to check on her and decided against it. If she was studying, he'd only disrupt her concentration. If she'd fallen asleep with the lights on, then he'd wake her up. Besides, it was none of his business. But he couldn't shake the kernel of concern that rested in the back his mind. He felt a responsibility to watch out for her. As a friend, a neighbor and even a cop.

Tossing the remote onto the coffee table, he stared

blindly at the flat screen, fully aware of the real reason behind his concern. He liked Carrie Fletcher. A lot. Too much. He kept telling himself it was because she was so kind to Jack and that they were partners in caring for him until the truth about his parentage was settled. But Carrie was quickly seeping into his system and touching places in his heart he'd long sealed up.

He'd sworn off relationships after Tiff. He'd learned two things about himself during his time in Vegas: he was susceptible to a certain type of woman, and he didn't have what it took to be a good husband. Whatever had made his dad the perfect family man hadn't been passed to him. Now that he knew about Jack, he was even more determined to steer clear of romance.

If he was going to be a good father to Jack, then he had to concentrate solely on him. Ideally, Jack should have a mom, someone to show him the kind of nurturing only a woman could provide. Someone like Carrie. But, after he'd bared his soul today and told her the truth about Tiff, she'd pulled away. Watching her barriers go up had been painful.

Her attitude had been still cool and distant when he'd picked Jack up after work. She hadn't invited him in or shared news about Jack's day. She quickly gathered up Jack's things and said goodbye. No doubt Carrie had dropped him back into the *questionable* category. He'd be fortunate to maintain their friendship. Hopefully, her opinion of him hadn't dropped too far, because he still needed her help with Jack. He'd have to find a way to restore their relationship and remind her of their deal. He'd help with the picnic in exchange for her help with Jack.

More importantly, he needed to keep his focus and remember that this attraction he was harboring for Carrie was inappropriate and pointless. It was simply a result of his insecurities regarding Jack and being dropped into fatherhood. Carrie was his anchor. Once his parentage was established, he'd feel more confident. Besides, neither one of them was looking for romance. He had his new career to concentrate on and Carrie would eventually get her degree and move on. So why did that thought leave a cold spot in his chest?

He still had no answer when he left for work the next day. It would take some time to adjust to his new schedule. Going to work at noon and getting off at eight cut into his time with Jack. He'd hoped to spend his mornings with his son, but the little guy really loved school and didn't want to miss it. That meant he'd have to make the most of his days off. At least they could have breakfast together before preschool started, but the long, quiet mornings alone gave him too much time to think and revisit regrets.

He was relieved when it was time to go to work. Phil greeted him in the parking lot as he was heading out for duty.

"So why didn't you tell me that Carrie Fletcher was your neighbor?"

"No reason I should."

"I hear you're hanging out at her place in the evenings after work. You two have a thing going on?"

Phil could make the most innocent situation into something inappropriate. Seth weighed how much to acknowledge. If he didn't answer, Phil would only grow more curious. "We're not involved. She's babysitting Jack until my shift ends."

"Nice. And does that include being her gofer for the picnic?"

What was he angling for? "How did you know about that?"

Phil grinned. "Come on, man. You know how news travels in this town. Got to hand it to you. That was a clever way of spending more time with the lovely lady."

"I volunteered to help with the picnic to repay her. Nothing more."

"Guess I should have tried that and maybe she wouldn't have turned me down."

"You asked her out?"

"Yeah, and she gave me the brush-off at hyperspeed. I guess I didn't have the right pedigree. No use competing with a Montgomery."

The thought of Carrie dating Phil didn't sit well. Phil was a decent-enough guy at heart, but he had a chip on his shoulder, and he could get testy when he didn't get his way. Not the kind of man someone sweet and sensitive like Carrie should be involved with. He felt better knowing she had refused Phil's invitation.

Seth set his jaw. "Carrie's not like that."

Phil crossed his arms over his chest and leaned back against the patrol car. "You sure about that? Are you sure you can trust her with your kid? I mean, I know she works for the church and all, but what else do you know about her?"

"All I need to know." Seth had had enough of this conversation. He reached for the door handle, but Phil didn't budge.

"So then you know she changed her name when she turned twenty-one?"

Seth's gut kicked. "How would you know that?"

"I checked. I figured you'd want to know who was watching your kid."

More likely Phil was trying to get back at him for Carrie turning him down. Phil took advantage of any chance to knock Seth down a peg.

"I know. And I'd appreciate it if you stayed out of my business. Carrie is a friend and I trust her."

A sardonic grin spread across Phil's face as he straightened. "Just looking out for you, pal. I'd hate to see you tangled up in a bad situation."

"I can look out for myself. Jack and Carrie, too. So you can stop worrying."

Seth climbed into his cruiser, started the engine and pulled out. Was Phil telling the truth or was he trying to get a rise out of him because Carrie had rejected him? If she'd changed her name, he knew she must have had a very good reason and he was certain it didn't involve anything illegal. He wouldn't let Phil's jealousy plant suspicions in his mind about Carrie.

Dispatch relayed a call from a man reporting his car stolen. The address was only a few miles away. He accepted the call and took the next turn to the east, grateful for the distraction. He needed to get the image of Phil and Carrie together out of his mind.

The rest of the week passed by quickly. Carrie managed to catch up on her regular projects and, thanks to Seth's help with the pony rides, check off another item from her list of events for the big picnic. Or course, that still left a dozen things to finalize and countless small details to address. Despite Seth's role as her assistant, she'd yet again resisted calling him for help, but sooner or later she'd have to ask him to lend a hand.

At the moment however, she had a more important obligation. Closing her laptop, she shut off the lights in her office, picked up her bag and headed toward the child-care center at the back of the building. A bubble of excitement began to swell deep inside. The highlight of her day this week had been picking Jack up from after-school care and taking him home with her. She was already feeling like one of the mothers waiting to pick up her child, and she'd learned being a single mom was harder than she'd thought. Jack was a nonstop bundle of energy. The time she used to spend after work relaxing was now filled with games, reading books, playing with toys and watching an animated movie about little cars.

Spending the evenings with Jack this week had only deepened her affection for the child. She'd purchased a car seat so Seth didn't have to switch them out. She'd also bought a few special toys for Jack to keep at her house, and stocked up on his favorite foods. A small voice had warned her that she was crossing into dangerous territory, but she'd do anything for Jack.

"Miss Carrie." Jack raced toward her when he saw her at the door. She had to remind him to retrieve his backpack. He chatted about school all the way home. After being so withdrawn those first days, he'd become a little magpie. She took comfort from the knowledge that he felt safe and cared for with Seth. And her. But she wanted more. She wanted to know for certain that he was Seth's son, though anyone who watched them for more than a few moments could tell they were related. But she knew how the system worked. Seth needed proof and the blank line on the birth certificate had been a blow.

The skies were darkening as she drove home, and she hoped they'd reach the house before the storm hit. Jack announced that he was hungry the moment they stepped inside her kitchen, and the storm announced its arrival at the same moment. She set to work preparing supper. She'd fallen into a pattern this week. First, she prepared a meal and fed Jack immediately. She chose recipes that could be easily reheated when Seth arrived later. Jack was free to play until close to eight o'clock, when Seth got off duty. At that point, she bathed Jack, dressed him in his pajamas and settled him into quiet play or looking at a book. When Seth arrived, she and Seth ate together and discussed the day. She enjoyed catching him up on the cute things Jack said and the progress he was making in preschool. They'd developed a comfortable relationship. Too comfortable, she worried, but she was committed to helping Jack.

A tap at her back door drew her quickly to the kitchen to let Seth in. The rumble of thunder sounded outside and a rush of cool damp air invaded the house as Seth hurried inside, his male presence instantly changing the feel of her home. He smelled like outdoors and leather, and there was a warmth about him she couldn't ignore. Not merely his body temperature, but a warmth of spirit. He was a nice man. An attractive man. Raindrops clung to his dark hair, and she fought the impulse to reach up and brush them away, wondering what his slightly wavy hair would feel like.

She lowered her eyes as a rush filled her cheeks. She should not be thinking things like that. Jack raced toward his father. "I missed you today, Pop."

Seth scooped him up in a big hug. "I missed you, too, Jack."

The sight of the little boy wrapped in the arms of the big man filled her with a sensation that stung the back of her eyes. They were so sweet together. She prayed they would be able to remain together no matter what the tests revealed. It was obvious that they needed each other.

Jack wiggled out of Seth's grasp. "Come see the tower I made. It's really big." He stood on tiptoe and stretched his arm as high as it would go. "Then I smashed it over and it made a big mess. *Goosh.* It was funny. But I made a new one and it's bigger."

Seth chuckled. "It's more fun to knock it down, isn't it?"

Jack nodded vigorously, clutching one of the brightly colored wooden blocks in his hand. During his time with Seth, he'd slowly eased his hold on the metal truck and begun playing with other toys, though he had latched on to the stuffed dog Seth had brought him that first night.

"Come watch me, Pop." Jack tugged at Seth's hand.

"You go ahead. I'll be right there. I want to talk to Miss Carrie for a minute."

Jack ran into the living room and Carrie turned to find Seth looking at her with a puzzled expression. "What?"

"He's a handful. I know watching him has been a big adjustment."

She shrugged. "I like having him around. He keeps me entertained." She sensed he was going to say more and she quickly changed the subject. "How was work today?"

He exhaled a slow sigh, his shoulders lowering a bit. "Routine until around six. We had a domestic disturbance to deal with."

"Aren't those dangerous?"

"They can be. That's why I called for backup. You just never know what can happen."

A shiver of alarm chased down her spine. She'd been so blinded by the negative image of him as a police officer that she'd never really thought about the danger he was exposed to on a daily basis. It gave her a whole new perspective on cops. All her life she'd seen them as heartless, unfeeling. Now she saw them as men who had families who loved them, who put their lives on the line each day.

How would she feel if something happened to Seth while he was on duty? She closed her eyes, refusing to let those kinds of thoughts into her mind.

Lightning flashed outside, jerking her attention back to the meal she'd prepared. She carried the plates to the table. Outside, the storm rolled on with a loud clap of thunder. Seth glanced over at her. "This is a nice way to end a workday. A hot meal with a friend on a stormy night."

Carrie saw his cheeks flush pink. The implications must have occurred to him, too. They were behaving like a family. Only they weren't.

Seth cleared his throat. "So you promised to fill me in on your big plans for the picnic?"

Another boom of thunder gave her a moment to regroup. "I mentioned that I want this to be like an old-fashioned picnic. But I'll also have setups for volleyball, baseball, cornhole toss and horseshoes. We have a band scheduled to play, a few carnival games, craft stands—oh, and the airplane."

"Airplane?"

She nodded. "Vern Bailey has a restored historic plane from WWII that he's going to bring to the park for the kids to see. You know, during WWII there was a pilot-training center here in Dover."

"I know. The airfield was where the municipal complex and the attendance center are now. That's a fun idea. It'll remind everyone of our history. The seniors will love it and the kids will, too."

"That's what I thought."

"You've done a great job putting this together. There's something for everyone. But it's a big job. Why haven't you asked me for more help?"

Carrie shrugged. "I haven't really needed to until

now. I've requested a map of Friendship Park so I can start figuring out where to position everything. Then I'll have to visit the park soon and make sure the space will work and the location is suitable for each event. I could use your help with that."

"Sure thing. Let me know when. Jack would enjoy the park." Seth pushed to his feet. "Speaking of Jack, I'd better get him home to bed."

Carrie followed, stopping under the arch to the living room, where Jack had fallen asleep on the floor with Leo. The little dog raised his head as if warning them to be quiet. "Poor little man."

Seth started forward. A loud pop resonated through the house and the lights went out.

Fear exploded in her chest, stealing her breath. She dropped the glass in her hand and heard it shatter on the floor. She yelped, burying her face in her hands. The darkness closed in, stealing her air.

She turned and bumped into solid warmth. She screamed and pushed away.

Strong hands grabbed her arms. She fought to pull free. "Carrie, it's okay. It's only a power outage. It'll probably be back on in a few minutes."

"Lights. I have to find the flashlights." The blood pounded in her ears.

"Here."

Light from his cell phone chased away some of the darkness and took the hard edge off her fear. She sucked in a shallow breath and gripped the phone with shaking fingers. Fighting a wave of humiliation, she avoided his gaze, turning back into kitchen and fumbling in the drawer for the large flashlight she kept there. Once it was on she could breathe a bit easier. "Is Jack okay?"

"Sound asleep. I'm sure he won't even know the lights went out. I'm more worried about you. You're shaking like a leaf. Are you afraid of the dark?"

She turned away from him. "No. Yes. A little."

The lights flashed back on, and Carrie sagged against the counter.

"You'd better sit down. You're pale as a sheet." Seth wrapped his arm around her shoulders and guided her toward the table. He cleaned up the broken glass, retrieved another one, filled it with water and set it in front of her.

Carrie wrapped her fingers around the tall glass, but her hand shook so much that she had to put it down again. Why did this happen every time the lights went out? She knew the reason, but why couldn't she get over it?

Seth reached out and took her hand in his, the contact draining off more of her fear. She squeezed tight, needing the comfort.

"You want to talk about it?"

How much could she tell him without opening up a topic she didn't want to share? She knew Seth well enough that he wouldn't take a flippant response. He'd press until he knew the truth. She just couldn't tell him who had done it to her.

"I got locked in a closet when I was twelve years old. Ever since then I've been terrified of the dark."

"How long were you in there?"

"Eighteen hours."

"Is that why you always have every light in the house on?"

She nodded. "Silly, huh? I've tried to get past it, but when the lights go out, I panic. I have big flashlights in every room and I replace the batteries religiously. I even sleep with a light on in my room every night."

"That explains why your place always looks like the neighborhood lighthouse."

His teasing and understanding wiped away the last of her fear. "I know I should be over it by now, but…" She shrugged. "Thank you for understanding." The look in his eyes enveloped her emotions, tugging her toward his warmth. His strong fingers tightened around hers, making her feel safe and protected. His nearness made it seem as if they were all alone, in another place entirely. If Seth was with her all the time, she might actually get over her phobia. There would be nothing to fear with him at her side.

Reality punctured the dreamy sensation. She tugged her hand from his. This couldn't happen. "I think the rain might be letting up." She stood and took her glass to the counter.

Seth followed, stopping at her side. Every sense in her body was attuned to his solid presence, and the compelling scent of him. It would be so easy to rest her head against his broad chest and put her arms around his waist. She dared a glance.

He placed his hands on her shoulders and angled her to face him. "Are you sure you're going to be all right?"

A sudden boom of thunder made her jump toward him. He pulled her into his embrace, his hand stroking her hair. "I think this storm might last all night. The power could go out again."

"I'll be fine." She held up the giant flashlight. "I have these everywhere."

He brushed her hair away from her temple. "I'm sorry you had to go through such a frightening ordeal. No child should be left alone in the dark."

Unable to resist, she wrapped her arms around him, letting them slide up the muscled back. She wanted to remain there, safe in his arms. But she wasn't safe. Not with him. She moved away, missing the warmth of his embrace. But when she looked into his eyes, she couldn't look away. Their gazes mingled together in mutual attraction. His hand came to rest on the side of her neck, turning her insides to melted butter.

"Carrie."

He said her name like a whispered prayer. She looked into his eyes and saw her own feelings reflected in his cobalt gaze. She stepped back and looked away. She had to be strong. For both their sakes. "Seth, maybe we should get a few things clear. I'm not looking for a relationship. Between my studies and my job, there's just no time for anything else."

She dared a look at Seth. He nodded, his face devoid of any discernible expression. Was he upset or relieved?

"I know. I'm not in any position to get involved, either. With my new job and Jack to think of, I've got all I can handle." His gaze softened, and he tapped her nose lightly with his finger. "But I can always use a good friend."

"Me, too."

Thunder rumbled across the sky. "I'd better get the little guy home to bed. Are you sure you're going to be all right?"

She nodded, wrapping her arms around her waist to keep from reaching out and hugging him again.

"Are you sure? Because I'm not leaving until I see you smile. Then I'll know you're really all right."

His gentle teasing had the desired effect. She smiled, and her heart skipped a beat when he returned it with his dazzling smile. Their gazes locked and she didn't try to look away. She liked looking at him, watching the fascinating planes of his face move and shift as he spoke. His twinkling eyes, with the little laugh lines, and his generous mouth, bracketed with deep dimples, never failed to capture her attention and evoke an appreciative sigh from her.

"There it is. Okay, Sunshine, I'm going to take Jack and leave, but promise you'll call me if you need me? Lights off or not. Deal?"

"Deal."

The moment the door shut behind Seth and Jack, Carrie felt the stark loneliness of her cottage. She busied herself with cleaning up, then tried to study, but her nerves were still on edge from the power outage. She'd revealed another piece of her past to Seth. Little by little she was allowing him to get closer. Too close. Shoving aside the memory of being in his arms, she prepared for bed, but once under the covers she could no longer deny her attraction. She was losing her heart to the man with the killer smile and caring nature.

She had to find a way to fight these feelings because falling for Seth was a very, *very* bad idea.

Chapter Six

Sunday morning. Seth convinced Carrie to sit with him and Jack for the late service. It had taken a little persuasion and his best smile, but she'd finally agreed. To be honest, it was probably more Jack's begging that had done the trick and not his smile.

Now that they were here, he found it hard to concentrate on the sermon. He'd been vividly aware of her nearness. Each breath he inhaled was mingled with her sweet perfume, and the brush of their shoulders as they stood for the hymns sent little tingles along his nerves. She sang with conviction and raw emotion, as if embracing every word.

He wanted to know how she was faring after the power outage the other night. As far as he knew, the lights had stayed on throughout the rest of the storm. Learning about her childhood experience had unleashed a powerful protective instinct in him. He wanted to keep her safe from not just from the dark, but anything that frightened her—the way he wanted to protect Jack.

But his need to shield Carrie felt very different. In fact, all his emotions where Carrie was concerned were new to him. It was an uncomfortable sensation and he wasn't sure he liked it at all.

When Reverend Jim began the sermon, Seth had to resist the impulse to rest his arm across the back of the pew. It was a possessive gesture he shouldn't risk. Carrie wouldn't appreciate it. Spending so much time together was becoming a huge distraction. He thought about her too often while at work, and couldn't take his eyes off her when they were together. Her sunny smile flashed through his mind at the most inopportune times. He'd told himself it was only natural to be drawn to Carrie. She was a beautiful woman with a sweet nature and a caring heart. Every night this week she'd had a hot meal waiting when he came to pick up Jack after work. He'd never questioned coming home to his empty cottage and tossing a frozen dinner into the microwave. Now he looked forward to Carrie's welcoming smile and a little boy's exuberant bear hugs. It was a life he'd never imagined, but one he could get used to.

The thought forced him to address the other moment with Carrie. He'd almost kissed her. He would have if she hadn't backed away. He'd wanted to for a long time now, but denied the impulse. Carrie was a friend. He had enough complications in his life without trying to deal with a relationship. But Carrie drew him in with her irresistible smile, her bright eyes and her caring nature. He'd never known anyone like her.

Seth struggled to concentrate on the sermon and still zoned out for most of it. He'd have to take time this week to go back and listen to it on the church website when it was posted. One comment, however, took root in his thoughts. The pastor warned against seeking forgiveness from the Lord, but not forgiving ourselves. He pointed out how easy it was to rehash our sins and wallow in regret instead of handing the issue over to the Lord. Giving up control, even of our guilt, was hard to do. It was easier to keep carrying our mistakes with us and nurturing the shame, thinking we were somehow making up for what we'd done. The words caused him to squirm in his seat and dredged up an emotion he wasn't ready to examine.

Settled in the truck after the service, Seth steered away from the square and took Peace Street out of town toward the south. He braced for Carrie's reaction when she realized they weren't going back to the cottages. His conscience stung a bit. He should have told her what he was planning, but he'd been afraid she'd turn him down.

"Where are we going?"

He gave her his best smile. "It's a surprise." The light in her eyes dimmed.

"Seth, I'm not fond of surprises. What's going on?"

"I'm bringing you home to meet the family." Too late he realized how that might sound. "My mom invited you to Sunday dinner."

"Oh. No. I can't do that. I'm sorry."

The look of alarm on her face puzzled him. "It's only dinner."

"You should have warned me."

"I was afraid you'd say no. Besides, my mom is anxious to meet you and thank you for helping with Jack.

She also told me I'd be grounded for a year if I didn't bring you along."

That brought a small smile to her face.

"I like to be prepared for things. I would have dressed differently."

"Don't you mean you would have had time to come up with a better excuse?"

She looked away, confirming his assumption.

"Carrie, why don't you like people?"

"I like people just fine. I work with them all the time in my job."

"Yes, but away from the church, you don't go anywhere or have any friends that I can tell."

"Are you keeping tabs on me?"

"I live next door. I notice things. It's what I do. Observe."

A muscle in her jaw flexed. "Are you speaking as a man or a police officer?"

"Both."

She played with the hair at her ear. "I work hard. When I come home, I'm tired and I have studying to do. That doesn't leave much time for socializing. I go out. Kathy and I have lunch now and again."

"So why don't you want to meet my family?"

"I do. But I'm not good with strangers or in groups. I never know what to say."

Was she serious? She was warm and friendly and everyone liked her immediately. He reached over and squeezed her hand. "Don't worry. It'll be fine. My family is easy to be around. No pressure. Just be yourself. Besides, you're going to love my mom's cooking."

Carrie sent a stern look in his direction. "Fine. But I reserve the right to be taken home on a moment's notice."

It was an odd request. "Deal. But I know that once you've met everyone, you'll want to hang around."

He noticed Carrie had clasped her hands tightly together in her lap. Was she really that anxious about meeting new people? Phil's comment reared its ugly head. Was Carrie hiding something? Is that why she didn't like to meet strangers and why she kept to herself? She did have an emotional fence around her, one in which she kept the gate firmly closed. But there was no way he'd believe that her fence was protecting something unlawful. He'd rubbed elbows with enough criminals, even in his short law-enforcement career, to know a decent person from someone hiding an ugly past.

Seth parked near the front door of the family home, a large sprawling structure that combined nineteenth century Victorian with Colonial Revival. The result was a stately mansion that fit perfectly in the oak-draped landscape.

"This is where you grew up?"

"Yep. Don't let the size fool you. It's just a house."

Carrie looked a bit pale and wide-eyed. "That is not just a house—that's a mansion. I had no idea the Montgomerys were so…"

"Blessed?" He chuckled. "Everyone has a preconceived idea of what we are." Seth hopped out and went around to open Carrie's door, then unbuckled Jack from the backseat.

"This is Grandma's house." Jack raced up the sidewalk and onto the porch in time to be greeted by a stately gray-haired woman who opened her arms and gathered the boy up into a hug.

Seth looked at Carrie. She stood stock-still, breathing rapidly. He took her hand. "Take a deep breath. I promise this won't hurt."

He led her up the stairs. "Mom, this is Carrie Fletcher."

"I'm so glad to meet you. I know we were introduced when you first came to work at the church, but I'm looking forward to getting to know you better. Seth and Jack talk about you all the time."

Seth beamed. "See. I told you it would be fine."

"Come on in and meet the rest of our clan."

Seth started to follow, but Carrie hung back. "What's wrong?"

"Can you take me home now?"

He wanted to reassure her again, but he had a feeling it wouldn't do any good. "Carrie, you're worrying about nothing. I'll be with you every moment."

Jack darted out onto the porch. "Hurry, Miss Carrie, we're going to eat, and Grandma is going to let me feed Champ."

Seth took Carrie's arm. "You don't want to miss the feeding of the dog, do you?"

She gave him a skeptical glance, but stepped forward. He made a mental note to stay close until she felt comfortable.

As they entered the house Seth took her hand, feeling a little like a parent taking a child to their first day of school. Except he couldn't imagine what she was afraid of. She was bright, capable and warm. He'd seen her handle the committee members as they organized the picnic, heard others talk about how good she was with people. Her reaction didn't make sense. She'd shared a lot about her childhood and how difficult it had been. Whatever was holding her back must have something to do with that. He wanted to know. He wanted to help.

He wanted to make it all better somehow.

The moment Carrie stepped inside the house, she knew she should have insisted Seth take her home. The foyer was imposing. Burled-wood panels, coffered ceiling and intricate wainscoting were on display everywhere. The place looked like a museum, not a family home. Except, it didn't feel like a museum. The atmosphere was warm and welcoming. Seth guided her into the large kitchen, where a dozen people were gathered around the massive island.

She stopped in her tracks, reluctant to meet the members of one of the oldest and most revered families in Dover. Still, she couldn't deny she was curious to meet the family Seth talked about with such pride and that had produced such a strong and caring man. Her biggest fear was doing something that would embarrass him, and draw attention to the fact that she was from a very different background and couldn't possibly fit in.

He steadied her with his hands on her shoulders. "Y'all, this is Carrie." A sea of faces looked at her, all smiling. A chorus of welcomes filled the air.

Seth's mother motioned them forward. "We're almost ready to sit down. I decided to make Grandma's fried chicken. Hope that's okay. Seth, honey, why don't you make the introductions, then we'll eat."

Carrie forced a smile as Seth moved to her side. "That big guy over there is Linc. He thinks he's the head of the family since he's the oldest, but he's really not." Everyone chuckled. "That's his wife, Gemma, and their son, Evan, and baby Sara. And the German shepherd is Champ."

"I got to feed him, didn't I, Evan?"

The older boy chuckled. "Yep."

Seth gestured toward the left. "This serious-looking dude is my brother Gil and his wife, Julie, and that cutie is my niece Abby. And you might have noticed there are more Montgomerys on the way. Twins."

"Boys." Evan nodded happily.

Another little girl entered the dining room and took a seat. "Don't forget about us, Uncle Seth."

"Not a chance. The one with the green-bean casserole in her hands is my sister, Bethany, and behind her is her husband, Noah, and his daughter, Chloe. They're still newlyweds so you'll have to forgive the sappy looks they give one another."

Noah pointed a finger at him. "You'll get your turn, fella, and I'll be there to torment the daylights out of you."

Laughter filled the room as they all took their places and Seth's mother gave the blessing. A sense of warmth and camaraderie settled over the room. When the food was all passed, Carrie took the time to examine the family from under lowered lashes.

Seth's brothers were both handsome men—tall,

lean, with angular features. Seth was slightly shorter and more solidly built, and in her opinion the most handsome. She wondered which side of the family he took after. He obviously got his twinkling eyes and the espresso-colored hair from his mom. She stole a quick glance, appreciation warming her veins. He'd shed the lightweight sport coat he'd worn to church and rolled up the sleeves of his white shirt, revealing corded forearms. The emotions stirring inside as he looked at her were dangerous. Especially here in the presence of his family. She refocused on the people around the table.

There appeared to be a verbal shorthand at work as they talked. They teased each other about things that had happened as children, how work was going and reminisced about their dad. And underneath it all was this obvious affection. Everyone made sure to include her in the conversation and ask about her work. They also expressed thanks for her help with Jack, which made her uncomfortable. Julie was particularly interested in her desire to go into social work.

She'd never experienced anything like it before. Adults, laughing, poking fun, but all in the spirit of love. It was enchanting and frightening at the same time. Part of her wanted to believe it was real, but another part of her waited for the arguments to begin.

To her surprise there was nothing pretentious about any of the Montgomerys. His mother, Francie, was warm and friendly, his brothers and new brother-in-law joked and laughed. The ladies in the family were a different story. They'd been sweet and reached out to her kindly, but she couldn't help comparing herself to them. Gemma was a charming strawberry blonde who clearly adored her family. Julie was a bundle of energy with a big smile that made you like her immediately. Bethany was an elegant beauty who had eyes only for her new husband and daughter.

They had perfect lives, normal lives, and from what she'd seen, they'd grown up in this glorious home with unconditional love and encouragement. How could she possibly understand or fit in with people like this? Yet, she was captivated by the family dynamic and found herself aching to be part of something so special, and envious of the life they'd been blessed with.

From somewhere deep inside a new emotion emerged. She wanted to be part of the happy scene, to be absorbed into the welcoming happiness, but she wasn't sure how to do that.

As the family dispersed after the meal, Carrie's anxiety spiked. She went in search of Seth. It was time to go home. She found him in the yard playing with his nieces and nephews and their dogs. He looked up when he saw her step onto the porch.

"Hey. You okay? Come down and meet the other dogs. Abby's Ruffles. And Chloe's new pup, Skittles. I'm afraid Jack is going to start begging for a real dog now instead of being content with Barky."

"I think I need to go home. I have some studying to do." It was a lame excuse and she could see the doubt and disappointment bloom in his eyes.

He came toward her, meeting at the bottom of the steps. "But you haven't had dessert yet. You have to have a piece of mom's pecan pie. It's legendary."

"I'd really better go."

"How about a compromise? Let's let Jack play with the dogs a little longer and we'll take a walk."

She wanted to demand to be taken home, but the thought of being alone with Seth was too inviting. "Okay, but a short one. I really do have to study."

She fell into step beside him, a soft breeze stirring the leaves on the trees and kicking up the scent of spring. What was it about this man that eased her tension simply by being near? They strolled past a charming cottage and a garden on their way to a small stream gurgling over smooth stones.

Seth stopped near the water's edge and perched on a fallen log. "So what do you think of my family? Pretty amazing, huh?"

Carried pulled a leaf from a low-hanging branch and fingered the smooth foliage in her fingers. "I have to admit they aren't what I expected, especially after I saw the house you grew up in."

"Don't confuse a large house with wealth. My great-granddad built it. My family owns a successful business, Montgomery Electrical Contractors, and it has provided a good living for my family for decades, but none of us were Rockefellers. We're just working stiffs that happen to have a big house. My mom doesn't even live in it now. She lives in the small cottage you saw. Linc and Gemma live there now."

"Your sister and sisters-in-law are all very beautiful and accomplished."

"So are you."

Carrie's cheeks flamed. "I wasn't fishing for a compliment."

"I know. But it's true, nonetheless."

She pulled her gaze from his with effort. She couldn't let herself believe the appreciation she saw in the cobalt depths. That would be a dangerous mistake. She took a few steps toward the slow-moving stream. "It's beautiful here. I can understand why your great-grandfather chose it for his home." She brushed her hand over a flowering shrub. "I envy you your family. We never had a home after Dad left. My brother and I moved from one cheap rental to another." Stunned at how much she'd revealed, she pointed to the water. "How far does this go?"

"This stream flows the length of Mom's land and along my property, too. Well, it *used* to be my property."

Carrie faced him. "You have land here?"

"Not anymore." He stood, picked up a stone and tossed it into the stream. "Dad subdivided the property and gave each of us two hundred acres on our twenty-first birthdays."

"What happened?"

"I sold it to go to Vegas." Seth shoved his hands into his back pockets. "I wanted out of Dover. I felt like I'd been fenced in my whole life. Too many rules here, too many people telling me I couldn't do something because it was wrong or dangerous or sinful. I was so sure they were trying to keep me from having any fun and exploring the world. Anyhow, after college I tried working in the family business, but it wasn't for me. I told my dad I wanted a year off to see what the rest of the country had to offer. He didn't take to the idea. To be fair, things were tough at the company and it was a lousy time to leave, but I was choking to death here. We had a huge fight and I told him I was going to sell my property and go, anyway. He finally agreed. He even sold the land for me. I left, ended up in Vegas and lived it up until the money ran out." He glanced back at the river. "Now that I'm back here, I realize that what I thought was a fence was really a guardrail, put there to keep me from falling into the chasm." He shook his head. "But for the grace of God... I have a lot of things in my past I'm ashamed of."

Carrie moved to his side and slipped her hand in his. She knew exactly what he was feeling. "Everyone has things in their past they regret."

"From where I stand you have a lot to be proud of. You've overcome a tough childhood and made a wonderful life for yourself. And you've managed to keep a cheerful outlook and positive approach to everything."

"Thank you. But all I was doing was trying to survive." The hair on the back of her neck tingled. She gasped and spun around, searching the woods, but saw only trees and underbrush.

"Carrie? What is it?"

"I don't know." She wrapped her arms around her waist as protection against the chill that had raced up her back. "I thought someone was watching me."

"Out here? Maybe one of the kids. They like to explore along the water."

"No. This was different." She shivered. The uneasiness escalated rapidly to alarm. "Can you take me home now, please?"

"Sure. I'll leave Jack here and come back for him."

"Thank you." She spun on her heels and walked quickly through the yard, not stopping until she was buckled into the truck. Had someone been in the woods watching her?

Seth climbed into the truck, studying her closely. "Are you all right?"

"I'm fine. I'm being silly. It was probably just a strange noise. I'm not used to being in the woods."

She reached for the door handle as soon as Seth pulled up to the front of her house. "Thank you for inviting me to dinner. I really did like your family. I should have thanked your mom before leaving. I'll call her and explain."

"No need. I'll talk to her. But don't be surprised if she invites you again. Once you've met the Montgomerys, you're considered family from then on."

Carrie said goodbye and hurried into the house, soaking in the sense of peace and safety she always found there. She looked out the window as Seth drove off. He'd told her she was family now. Oh, how she wished that were true. She would like nothing more than to be part of a large, loving family like his. But how would they react if they knew the truth about her past?

She took her books out onto the front porch to study. She was deep into her work when the hair on her neck prickled again. She looked up. Her body tensed. The park across the street was filled with families, but she had the feeling someone there was watching her. No one looked familiar or threatening. Slowly her nerves relaxed. Maybe she was imagining things. There was no reason for anyone to be watching her. She was getting paranoid. It was nothing more than a case of nerves. Ever since Jack had arrived she'd been forced out of her comfort zone every moment. But she couldn't deny the joy and excitement the Montgomerys had brought to her life.

Somehow, she had to find a way to balance the old and the new, and still maintain her barriers.

She was beginning to think that might not be possible.

Seth pulled a T-shirt over his head and went to check on Jack, who was supposed to be brushing his teeth. Instead, he was floating the caps from the toothpaste tube, the mouthwash bottle and the top to Seth's shaving cream in the sink. The boy's imagination never ceased to amaze and amuse him. "Buddy, you're getting your pajamas all wet." He removed the caps and let out the water. "Brush those teeth, then let's get you into bed."

"But I'm not tired. I want to watch a movie. Miss Carrie showed me one about cars. Can we watch that one?"

Seth had no idea what he was talking about, but if it was something his son liked, he'd go find it ASAP. "Not tonight, buddy. You have school in the morning, and you need to get to sleep."

"Aw, Pop. I want to stay up with you."

Jack usually behaved without question, but he was wide-awake and showed no signs of being drowsy. But Seth was worn-out and he needed sleep, no matter how energized his son was.

"Jack. Teeth, then bed. Let's get with it." He hated that his stern tone put a frown on the sweet little face, but there had to be rules. He shook his head. He was beginning to understand his father better. Funny, how one little person could shift a grown man's entire perspective on life.

His phone rang from the living room. "You finish up and hop into bed. I'll be right there to tuck you in."

A few minutes later Seth ended the call and mentally restructured his plans for the next twenty-four hours, and it had to start with Carrie. She answered on the second ring.

"Seth? Everything okay?"

He liked the way she was always thinking about Jack and wanting to make sure he was all right. "Yes. It's all good. But I need to go back into work tonight. Brian Shipley's wife is in labor. It's his first kid and I told him I'd help him out. He works the night shift, which means I need to leave Jack with you if it's not too much trouble."

"Of course it's no trouble. Will he be okay here overnight, though?"

"I think so. You might have to let Leo sleep with him."

"No problem. See you shortly."

Seth took the small gym bag he'd purchased for Jack and starting packing. Jack would be with Carrie tonight and until his own shift ended tomorrow evening and maybe into another night. He'd need a little of everything.

"I'm sorry, Pop. I'll brush my teeth and I won't play in the sink anymore. Promise."

Seth looked at Jack. Big tears were rolling down his little cheeks, and his bottom lip quivered. He wasn't sure what had upset the child.

"I don't want to go away! I want to stay here with you."

Like a punch in the gut, Seth realized how his actions must look to Jack. He was packing his clothes. Jack must think he was sending him away. He should have explained things before he started throwing his clothes into the bag. He sank onto the bed and opened his arms. "Come here, son." Jack started to cry and Seth lifted him onto his lap and cradled him close. "I'm not sending you away, Jack. Not ever. And you've done nothing wrong. That phone call was from my job. I have to go back in and work until morning. You're going to sleep at Miss Carrie's tonight and maybe tomorrow night, too, until I get this special job done. Do you understand?"

"You're not mad at me?"

"No. You're my little buddy. I love you. I didn't mean to scare you."

"Am I really going to sleep at Miss Carrie's house?"

"You are."

"Can Leo sleep with me?"

Seth chuckled and hugged him close. "I'm pretty sure he'd like that."

Jack scooted off his lap, a serious expression on his face. "Barky will want to come, too. He'll get sad if I leave him here." He dashed off to the other room, leaving Seth shaken and doubting his ability to raise a child.

He should have thought ahead and spoken to Jack first. He hadn't connected the dots between his stern reprimand and packing the suitcase. Poor little guy must have been terrified.

The sudden change in his schedule forced him to think again about his odd work hours. Carrie was a blessing, but he couldn't impose on her forever to help out with Jack. His mother would gladly watch Jack, but he was determined to be a hands-on dad. Unless, of course, Jack wasn't his, after all.

The thought twisted like a hot auger into his core. He couldn't let himself think that. Losing Jack would be like ripping out his heart, and he knew as sure as he drew breath that he would never recover. Ever.

Chapter Seven

Carrie helped Jack say his prayers, then tucked the covers snug around him. Leo quickly settled at his side. She'd decided to let the boy sleep with her in case the strange house and unfamiliar surroundings frightened him. She kissed his cheek. What would it be like to kiss her own children good night? To watch them say their prayers and be awakened to their happy faces each day. "Good night, Jack." She started out the door.

"Aren't you going to turn the lights out?"

Jack looked up at her from beneath the covers. Leo lifted his head, as if waiting for an answer, too. This was something she hadn't thought through when she'd agreed to keep Jack overnight. Lights. She sorted through her options. Jack was probably accustomed to sleeping with only a night-light. Not something she could do. She needed more than a faint glow from a tiny bulb. She moved to the nightstand and switched off the lamp. "How's that?"

Jack shook his head and pointed to the ceiling. "You have to turn off the ones up there."

No way. Not a chance. She'd never sleep if she did. She sat on the edge of the bed. "Jack, I have a secret. I really don't like the dark. I usually sleep with all the lights on."

A thoughtful frown appeared on the child's face and his lips pressed together. "You could leave the bathroom light on and the one out there in the hall. Pop does that so I don't get scared."

It was a good compromise. Not perfect, but if she lay with her face toward the bathroom light she might be able to sleep. She'd try it for Jack's sake. "You are a very smart little man." She kissed his cheek, patted Leo, then walked to the door and switched off the overhead lights. Her stomach tightened, but her gaze rested on the boy. She wanted Jack to be able to sleep more than she wanted the feeling of safety for herself.

"Good night, Jack."

"'Night."

Curled up on the sofa, she let herself fantasize about a family of her own. It was something that was starting to occupy her thoughts more than it should. She understood that watching Jack, sharing suppers with Seth, had created a false family dynamic ripe with implications, but while it was fun to imagine, she knew it wasn't a future she could have.

Her cell phone rang and she glanced at the screen. Mavis. She accepted the call and settled back. "You must have known I needed to talk to you."

"You always say that when I call." The older woman's voice was thick with affection.

"Because I'm always thinking about you. You're family, Mavis."

"And you are the daughter I never had. How are things going? You still watching that little boy?"

Carrie caught her friend up on the events of the last few weeks. "What about you? How are things in Little Rock?" The silence on the connection caused a blip in her pulse.

"I wanted to let you know I got a call from the prison. Neil is up for parole next month. I thought you should know."

Ice water surged through her veins. "So soon?"

"Apparently he's been minding his manners. But that's no guarantee."

"What if he tries to find me?"

"We talked about this and it's why you changed your name. I know this is upsetting, but you'll be fine. You're a strong woman, Carrie. You've fought so many battles and won them all. I'm so proud of you."

Carrie spoke with Mavis a few minutes longer before hanging up. Her friend had done her best to reassure her that her brother, Neil, had no reason to look her up, and if he did, she'd moved and had a new identity. She was safe.

A shiver chased up her spine, reminding her of those odd moments when she'd thought someone had been watching her. It couldn't have been Neil. He was still incarcerated. But what if he was granted parole? Should she tell Seth? Should she stop watching Jack just to be safe? Hugging her knees up to her chest, she scolded herself for giving in to unwarranted fear. She was anticipating something that probably wouldn't happen. Mavis was right. She had a bad habit of falling prey to her fears. She was stronger than her past. God had forgiven her and established her in a new life. She had to trust that He would see her through whatever lay ahead.

Never in her wildest imaginings had she expected that getting one little boy up, dressed, fed and out the door to preschool was more difficult than organizing an entire citywide picnic. She'd arrived at the office frazzled and exhausted, but oddly filled with satisfaction. Jack's happy chatter on the way to school, his big hug and wave as she left him at the door to the preschool rooms would keep a smile on her face the rest of the day.

A few hours later, her smile was long gone as she hung up the phone and rubbed her forehead. Wanda Peters, the head of the food-donation committee, had called first thing this morning to say she had to resign. Her little granddaughter was seriously ill and Wanda needed to go to Atlanta to help. Carrie had been calling prospective replacements without success.

The donation of canned goods was the foundation of the picnic. Everyone who wished to attend had been asked to bring nonperishable food as their admission fee. With the large number of people expected, someone had to be in charge of organizing the collection point. So far, everyone she'd contacted was already busy with other things.

She looked up from her desk when someone called

her name. Francie Montgomery smiled as she came into the office. She wore a dressy pair of pants and a soft flowing blouse with a statement necklace and heels, the very image of the successful businesswoman she was.

"I hope I'm not interrupting you?"

"Not at all. I'm ready for a break. I'm trying to re-shuffle some people to work at the picnic." She gestured to the chair in front of her desk.

"Let me guess. Wanda's sudden departure to take care of her granddaughter?"

"Wow. News travels fast. It's left me with a dilemma. I need to find someone to handle the food donations the day of the picnic. She felt really bad about backing out, but her family needs her more than we do right now."

"Agreed. And that's why I'm here—to volunteer to take over her duties. In fact, the whole Montgomery family wants to step in and help out."

Carrie wasn't sure she'd heard correctly. "Are you serious? That would be wonderful. But it's a big job. You'd be tied up all day and wouldn't get to enjoy the picnic."

Francie waved off her concern. "There are a lot of us, so we can take turns. We have it all worked out. We receive dozens of boxes at the company every day, so Linc and Gil will start collecting the empties to hold the donations, and we have a large panel truck we can park nearby to store and lock the filled boxes. We'll also sort and deliver the food to the charities you've chosen."

Carrie breathed a sigh of relief. "Miss Francie, I can't thank you enough. This will make the transition so much easier. Wanda was a real blessing and she had all the details worked out. I wasn't sure I could find anyone to take over that job."

"We're happy to do it. The Montgomerys have been members of this church for generations. It's the least we can do. But now I need a small favor from you."

"Name it."

"I've already checked with my son, but I wanted to get the okay from you, too. I'd like to pick up Jack from preschool and take him home with me for the day. I try to schedule one-on-one time with my grandchildren so we can have our own special memories. I think Jack is finally comfortable enough to come home with me. We're going to make cupcakes and I've picked up that new animated movie. Evan wants to spend time with him, too. He's glad to have a new boy cousin. He's been complaining there are too many girls in our family. Seth won't have to pull double duty again since the Shipley baby has arrived, so he'll come by and pick him up later this evening."

"That's a wonderful idea, and I'm sure Jack will love being with you, but you didn't have to get my permission. I'm just his babysitter."

Francie's eyes softened. "No, Carrie. You're much more than that. Seth and Jack rely on you and trust you. I'm very appreciative of all you do for them."

The compliment warmed her heart. "It's my pleasure. They… Jack is a sweet little boy. I love having him with me."

"Well, I'm going to go get Jack and you can look forward to a nice quiet evening all alone. We can all use those from time to time."

"So true. Thank you."

Carrie's mood dimmed when Francie left her office. She'd told the truth. Jack would love spending special time with his grandmother and his cousin. But the prospect of going home without him left a hole in her chest. She looked forward to hearing him chatter about school and his friends on the way home. Leo would miss him, too.

However, Francie was right about needing alone time. Normally she would be delighted, since she was behind on a couple of her courses and could use the evening to catch up. Without Jack there, she'd be able to concentrate and probably finish up the one subject. But, oh, how lonely the cottage would feel. For a moment she even considered calling Kathy and suggesting a movie, but that was the coward's way out. She was a big girl. She could handle one night without her little fellow. After all, he wouldn't be with her forever.

Once she had her degree and became a certified social worker, she could work anywhere. Dover was a small town, and landing a job here would be difficult, which meant she would have to move to a bigger city.

The realization made her stomach sour. She'd never thought about her life after she graduated. It had always seemed so far away. A distant goal. She loved Dover, loved her job at the church and the people she worked with. It was where she'd like to stay.

She stood and went to the window. The goal ahead was blurred now. Not as sharp and clear as it had always been. Somewhere along the way, another goal had started to form. One where she had a man she loved and a child of her own. It had always been a fantasy, but now she was thinking it might just be a possibility.

The sun was just starting to lower on the horizon when Seth pulled into the long tree-lined drive of his family home. He steered the truck past the main house and pulled to a stop near his mother's cottage. He peered out the windshield. Something was different. His gaze landed on a huge play set that had been erected under the old oaks. A large fort rose above a slide, several swings, ladders and a half-dozen other accessories. Evan and Jack were popping in and out of the fort having a good time. Seth got out of the truck as his mom walked toward him. "When did that arrive?"

"Linc finished it this morning and the boys haven't left it since. I even had to feed them lunch out there." She smiled up at him. "You might have to get one in your backyard for Jack."

"My yard is too small. In fact, I'm beginning to think my whole house is too small. I may have to look for a new place."

"You mean like a family home?"

"Maybe. He takes up more space than I realized for such a little guy."

"And you might marry someday."

Was his mom turning into a matchmaker? "Not likely." Jack spotted him and waved from the fort, then started carefully down the ladder.

"Pop." Jack ran across the lawn so fast he fell down, but got up again and raced toward him. "I'm glad you're home. Did you see the humongous fort Uncle Linc built?

Isn't it big? And there's a rope ladder and a slide and swings, and we had lunch up there, too."

"So I heard."

Jack wrapped his little arms around Seth's neck and squeezed. Seth's heart swelled to the point of bursting from his chest. "Are you ready to go home?"

"I guess. Will Miss Carrie be there?"

"We'll call her and have her wave at the window. Leo, too."

"Yay!"

After a long goodbye that included lots of hugs for his grandmother, one for his cousin and one for the dog, they started for home. Seth was still exhausted from the night shift, so he opted for supper from the Fil-er-up Burger place.

Jack talked nonstop about his time with his grandmother, and it was a relief when he fell asleep beside Seth on the sofa. He'd begged for a few more minutes of playtime and Seth had relented. He'd missed his son more than he'd expected. He gently hugged the little boy closer to his side, placing a kiss on the top of his head. He could cheerfully remain like this forever and never let go.

Since Brian was filling in for him tomorrow, that meant he'd have three days off and lots of time to spend with Jack and maybe help Carrie with the picnic.

He'd missed Carrie, too. Working the night shift had made it impossible for him to connect with her. She'd been on his mind more than usual lately. Learning about her brother had left him feeling even more protective.

He suspected there was more to the story, but until she was ready to share, he'd have to be patient.

His cell phone blared into the quiet house, and he snatched it up before the sound could wake Jack. The number on his cell didn't look familiar and he almost ignored the call. He didn't know anyone in Cancun. But something urged him to answer. "Hello?"

"Seth? It's me. Tiff."

His heart stopped. "Tiff? How did you get my number?"

"I know where you live. And you can find anyone on the internet. I heard you were looking for me."

"I want to know about Jack."

"What about him?"

"Is he mine? You didn't put a father's name on the birth certificate."

"That's because I'm not sure who it is. You weren't the only guy near the end, you know. You'll have to do a test or something."

Seth rubbed his forehead, fighting the anger rising in his chest. "I *have*. I also want to know why you shipped him here, dumped him on my front porch and left him all alone with a note pinned to his chest."

"What? I didn't do that. I sent him with my friend Monique. She was supposed to hand him over to you and give you the note."

"He's just a little boy. How could you send him here like a package?"

"Because I was leaving the country. I finally found someone, Seth. He's handsome and rich and he thinks I'm special. He brought me here to Cancun and we're staying in a five-star luxurious resort. It all happened so fast I didn't have time to call you, so I sent him with Monique. I was in Beaumont at the time and she was heading to Fort Walton. Since she had to go right by Dover, I figured it would be okay."

Seth clenched his jaw to keep from cursing. "It wasn't okay and Dover is not exactly on the way. He arrived here dirty, hungry and scared. Did you know this woman? Was she a friend? Someone you could trust?"

"Yeah, of course. I mean, we'd known each other a few days."

"You left him with a stranger? How could you do that? What if she'd harmed him or abandoned him somewhere?"

"But she didn't, 'cause you have him now."

The indifference in her tone sliced to his core. How could she do such a heartless thing? He took a moment to calm himself. "I want to know the truth. When did you find out you were pregnant and why didn't you call me and let me know?"

"Stop badgering me. Why should I tell you? We'd already split up."

"And what about Jack? If the test proves he's mine, I plan on keeping him with me."

"Fine."

"Will you agree to full custody or maybe signing away your parental rights?"

"Sure. I won't have time for him from now on."

Seth gritted his teeth so hard his jaw ached. "I need his medical records, too, if you have them. How soon can you send those?"

"Don't get on your high horse. I've got it around some place. I'll send it when I can find it okay? Are we done?"

Seth ended the call, running his fingers through his hair. Emotions churning like a hornet's nest, he closed his eyes and inhaled a slow, deep breath. How had he ever have thought he loved her? How could she agree so easily to give up her child, and how could she send Jack on a road trip with a stranger?

He had hoped talking to Tiff would answer his questions, but all she'd done was muddy the waters and stir up his guilt. There'd been a time when he'd thought Tiff was the woman of his dreams. He saw now that those dreams were the product of an immature, naive young man who had no idea what he wanted and what was truly important. And he wasn't sure his judgment had improved. The few women he'd dated since that time hadn't been the forever type. They'd been the kind who weren't looking for commitment. He hadn't even realized it until he'd met Carrie.

His whole concept of the right woman had changed. He had no plans to get married again, but if there was a next time, he'd make sure she was smart, kindhearted, respectable and a believer. Someone like Carrie.

But how could he ask a woman like her to overlook his past? No matter how hard he tried, it would always follow him around like dirt stuck to his shoe.

He glanced down at the little boy still snuggled beside him. It was best if he and Jack went it alone. They'd be fine and he'd do everything necessary to give his son a life of love and happiness.

* * *

Carrie stretched her neck side to side to loosen the tightness, then leaned back in her office chair. From the moment she'd arrived at work today, she been chasing one problem after another. Returning phone calls, tracking down items needed for a ladies' luncheon this weekend and giving a visitor a tour of the church. Pastor Jim had requested a meeting about an event slated for next month that had to be rescheduled, then the Dover Parks department had called to say the official permit for the picnic was ready for pickup.

The parks office was in the old courthouse in the square. Peace Community stood on the northwest corner. It would only take a few minutes, but it was time she didn't really have. She was meeting with two of the committee chairmen shortly about picnic issues. She could really use Seth's help, but pulling him off duty for this was ridiculous. She'd have to risk missing her appointment and run to the old courthouse.

"Afternoon, little lady."

Like an answer to a prayer, Ralph appeared in her doorway. "Ralph, I am so glad to see you. Are you available to run a quick errand for me?"

"Sure am. What can I do for you?"

"The parks department is holding our official permit for the picnic. They'll be closing soon and I really need it today. Can you run over there and pick it up? Ask for Dick."

Ralph nodded and waved a hand in the air as he walked away. "On my way. Be back in a jiffy."

An hour later Carrie had just completed her committee meeting when Ralph peeked into her office. She'd expected him much sooner, but her door had been closed, so she assumed he'd been reluctant to interrupt. "Ralph. Thanks for doing this." She held out her hand, but Ralph frowned and rubbed his chin.

"Well, now, I seemed to have misplaced it."

"What? How could you misplace the permit between the courthouse and here?"

"I don't rightly recall. I saw Dick and picked up the paper. He put it in a nice blue envelope for me so it wouldn't get messed up. Then I started back here, and I ran into Billy Wilcox and we talked a bit. Then I came back here, but I didn't have the envelope. I went back and looked, but I didn't see it anywhere."

Carrie's heart sank. "Ralph, without the permit we can't hold the picnic. I'm not sure we can get another one in time. I suppose I could talk to the director and see if he will issue another one."

"I'm real sorry, Miss Carrie. I guess what they say about me is right. I'm too old for this job."

Her irritation faded. "No, Ralph. These things happen."

"What things?"

Carrie breathed a sigh of relief when she saw Seth step into her office. "What are you doing here?"

"Just passing by and thought I'd see how things were going."

Ralph twisted his ball cap in his hands, his head lowered. "I'm afraid I messed up good this time."

Carrie rested a hand on Ralph's shoulder as she explained.

"No problem, Mr. Ralph." Seth patted his narrow shoulders. "I'm good at tracking things down. Why don't you and I go see if we can find it? Someone must know where it is. We'll investigate."

Seth winked at Carrie as he ushered the older man out. Barely fifteen minutes later he reappeared, waving a big blue envelope. "Here you go."

"Where did you find it?"

Ralph lowered his head and looked at her through sad eyes. "I must have left it on the bench when I was talking to Billy. I forgot we sat there."

Seth smiled. "It was still there, just waiting to be found."

"Miss Carrie, I think I'd better turn over the assistant's job to Seth here. Full-time. I want to help, but I only seem to mess things up now. I'm sorry."

Carrie came out from behind her desk and gave Ralph a hug. "Nonsense. We need you, Ralph. You're important to the church. But I do have a suggestion if you're willing to listen."

The old man nodded.

"I thought it would be nice to have an official greeter at the picnic, someone to welcome the guests and direct them to the events and venues. No one is more welcoming or friendly than you. Would you consider becoming the church's greeter? Not just at the picnic but every Sunday."

A light bloomed in the pale eyes. "Yes, ma'am. I'd like that. I'd like that a lot."

Carrie watched Ralph walk away, then looked at Seth. His warm and tender gaze softened her insides.

He pulled her toward him and placed a gentle kiss on her forehead. "That was sweet. You have a way with people. You know how to make them feel valued and important. I'm blessed to have you as a friend."

The gesture left her weak and quivering inside, and she stepped back, struggling to keep her focus. She smiled and pushed the hair behind her ear. "You may not say that after next week. You might spend more time running errands than enforcing the law."

He chuckled. "Finally. I'm going to get to do some real picnic-assistant work. Go ahead, lay it on me."

"First, I have a meeting with the city parks manager tomorrow after lunch to go over the logistics of the picnic, discuss parking and mainly to make sure we have all the electrical power we'll need for the vendors and bouncy houses. Since you come from an electrical family, I could use your knowledge."

"No problem." He rested his hands on his duty belt. "Though you should be okay. Dover has several big events at the parks and the downtown square, and power has never been an issue."

"I'm also picking up a map of the park and I was hoping you'd help me decide the best locations for the various events. A second pair of eyes is always good."

"Great. I'll pick you up, and we'll go see the park manager. Then, afterward, we'll get Jack, grab some pizza and go to my place. We can sort it all out while we eat. Anything else?"

"I'll still need to visit the park and walk the areas to make sure they're suitable."

"Sounds like a day at the park is in order. We'll head

over there Saturday with Jack. He'll have a blast on that giant playground."

"Thanks, Seth. I really appreciate your help."

He held her gaze with his smiling eyes. "My pleasure."

She moved behind her desk. "Was there a reason you stopped by today?"

"Yeah." He ran a hand over his chin.

Carrie saw his eyes darken and prepared herself for bad news. "What happened?"

"My ex-wife, Tiff, called last night. She's in Mexico with her latest boyfriend, but the important thing is she's agreed to give up all rights to Jack."

"That's great."

"It is. Unfortunately, she couldn't tell me for certain that Jack is mine. So we're still back to waiting for the DNA-test results."

She moved back to his side and laid her hand on his arm. "I know it'll prove you're his father."

"Let's hope so. I'm not sure what I'll do if the test is negative."

She tightened her fingers on his arm, aware of the strength beneath her hand. "I'm praying every day that the results will be positive."

"Thanks, Carrie. It helps to know you're on my side. I'd better get back to work. Call me anytime for those errands."

A sense of loss settled on her shoulders the moment Seth disappeared from sight. Like him, her hopes had soared when he said his former wife had called. He hadn't gotten the answer he'd wanted and she hurt for him.

She wished she could do something other than pray. She knew it was the most important thing she could do, but sometimes it felt very inadequate. She knew God was at work in the situation, but she wanted to wrest control from him and force the outcome she wanted.

What she should be working on was rebuilding her protective barriers. Seth would be even more involved in her life now. The picnic was only weeks away and there was still so much to do, but spending more time with Seth made it harder to keep her feelings in check. On some level she suspected it was too late. She was falling in love with Seth, and one day soon she'd have to face the consequences.

Chapter Eight

Seth glanced out of the corner of his eye and watched Carrie as she studied the park map, searching for the perfect spot for each picnic event. Her brows were knit together, her teeth rested on her lower lip and her left hand toyed with the wavy hair behind her ear. She was the most adorable woman he'd ever met, and she smelled like summer.

He couldn't think of a better way to spend a Friday night. They'd agreed to work at his house tonight in case they went past Jack's bedtime, and they had. Jack had wanted to show Carrie his new toy racetrack that he could slide the little cars down. He'd played with little else since Seth had brought it home yesterday. By the time Jack had finished telling Carrie all about his room and his toys, it was bedtime. Seth had managed to get him into bed, but only after reminding him of the trip to Friendship Park the next day.

Now he sat at the dining room table with the map spread out and Carrie at his side. It was amazing how much warmth and softness she brought into his home. She was a woman he could easily fall for; in fact, he might have already begun to do exactly that. She occupied his thoughts more and more each day, and when he saw her with his son, his mind always filled with images of the three of them together. But he'd failed in every relationship he'd attempted, and he didn't want to fail with Carrie. She's been disappointed too much in her life. She must have sensed him watching her, because she jerked her head toward him.

"What?"

He grinned. "Have you sorted out all the spots?"

"I think so. I'm concerned about parking, though. We're taking up big sections of the parking area for the airplane and the pony trailer and truck."

"What about a shuttle service from the church to the park?"

She nodded. "That's a great idea, but we'd have to hire buses and I'm not sure our budget can handle the cost."

"Not buses. Little shuttle wagons designed to carry people. I keep forgetting you haven't been in Dover very long, so you don't know about the Founder's Day Celebration we have each fall on the square. It's a really big deal. One of the main events is the hot-air-balloon race. It's held in a field on the edge of town, and Virgil Hall uses his wagons to shuttle folks from downtown to the launch site. I'll contact him tomorrow."

"All that leaves is to visit the park and make sure we've chosen the right locations for everything."

"We'd better go early. I don't think Jack will be able to contain himself if we wait too long."

"I'll be ready after breakfast." She searched his gaze a moment. "Have you heard from Tiff again? Did she send you any information about Jack?"

"No. But it's only been a few days." He rested his elbows on the table, old regrets rushing out before he could stop them. "I always believed what I did wouldn't affect other people. I never stopped to consider how my choices would impact the people around me. Now I see that I hurt my parents when I left Dover, and I hurt Tiff by presenting myself as something I wasn't, then leaving her alone. I hurt myself by choosing to live against my values, and mostly I hurt Jack by not being part of his life."

Carrie slipped her hand in his. "But you're doing the right thing now. You're a wonderful father, Seth."

"I want to be. Jack deserves nothing less." He looked into her beautiful eyes, the color of a summer sky. "You are a ray of sunshine in all of this. I would have been lost without you. Jack, too."

"You would have done fine."

"I don't know about that. I've always looked at marriage as a serious commitment. I took a vow before God, but I didn't take into consideration what He might think of the woman I chose. It's who I wanted and I expected Him to jump on board and bless my choice."

He ran a hand through his hair. "I've spent my life chasing the wrong kind women. All I want now is a woman who's caring and strong and honorable." He laid his hand on hers. "A woman of strong faith."

The look on Carrie's face sent a chill through him. Her eyes were wide with alarm; her lips were pressed tightly together and her skin was pale. She was obviously distressed by the things he'd said to her. Of course, a woman like Carrie would find his past behavior abhorrent. He'd been a fool to spill his guts like that. Maybe he could explain. "Carrie…"

She pushed back from the table and stood, folding up the map. "I'd better go. It's late."

Seth followed her to the door. "Look, Carrie I didn't mean to unload on you like that."

"It's all right. I understand."

"Are we still on for tomorrow?" Seth held his breath. There was a long pause before she answered. He'd really screwed up this time.

"Sure. I'll be ready."

Seth closed the door, kicking himself for his stupidity. He may have just sabotaged the first relationship that really mattered to him. Not only had his past caught up with him, but his rebellious nature might have killed any hope he had with Carrie.

Carrie waited at the bottom of the tall slide in the playground of Friendship Park the next morning, ready to catch Jack as he came down. The little boy was eager to experience the slide, but had gotten scared halfway up the ladder. Seth had helped him to the top, where he now sat, his hands clutching the handles, his eyes wide with anxiety and expectation while she encouraged him to let go and sail down the shiny silver chute. She saw Seth whisper something in his ear. Jack nodded, then let go, whizzing downward and landing with his little feet on the ground and right into Carrie's waiting arms.

"You did it! Wasn't that fun?"

Jack nodded rapidly, a huge smile on his face. "I want to do it again." He raced around to the ladder and got a hug and whirl-around from Seth.

"Good job, buddy. You are a brave little boy. You want me to go up with you again?"

"No, Pop. I can do it." He grabbed the handrails and made his way to the top, only slowing slightly on the last few rungs. He sought a reassuring glance from Seth before pushing off and flying downward again.

Seth chuckled and joined Carrie as they watched Jack tackle the slide a few more times. "Can you believe he's the same quiet little boy you found that night?"

"No. I'm amazed at how quickly he's adjusted. But that's all because of you. He knows you love him and he responds to that."

"I hope so."

"Thank you again for all your help last night figuring out where these events should be set up, and I'm especially grateful for your idea about a shuttle service."

"I put in a call to Virgil first thing this morning about it, and he was a bit offended no one had asked him sooner."

"I would have if I'd known." She grinned. "I never expected you to be so valuable. Pony rides, shuttles and power expertise. You are a man of many surprises."

"So now you like surprises?"

She liked him. "Sometimes. But not right now. We

still have to check to make sure the sites we've picked will actually work."

"Then let's get at it."

It took some coaxing, but they finally got Jack interested in seeing the rest of the park, and he took full advantage of the wide-open spaces to run and tumble. Using the map, they walked through every section of the large park to check its suitability. Seth had brought a tape measure so they could measure how many vendor wagons and booths they could fit into the designated locations.

Seth rested his hands on his hips. "It looks like you'll have more than enough space to set up. All that leaves is the pony ride, and I don't think our original idea will work so well."

"No. I think we put it too close to the food vendors." She pinched her nose and grimaced.

Seth chuckled. "Right. Pony smells and food smells are not a good combination."

"Maybe we could tuck it away near the edge of the field. It'll be seen but not smelled." She gave him a wink.

"That should work. I'll measure it to make sure it's large enough."

Seth had just finished his assessment of the proposed pony-ride area when his phone rang. He answered, his expression tense and wary. Carrie met his gaze but he looked away, walking off a few yards as he conversed. A dozen bad possibilities surged into her mind. Did it have something to do with Jack? Had his mother changed her mind and wanted him back? If that were true, she couldn't imagine the heartache Seth would endure. He loved the little boy, and he'd invested his whole being into caring for him. Losing Jack would destroy him.

And her, too. She swung her gaze to Jack, who was stooped down near a big tree, examining something on the ground. He'd become so much a part of her life. She pushed aside the disturbing thoughts. She was jumping to conclusions all because of a look on Seth's face. It could be a call about work, some police matter he didn't want to deal with or anything at all other than Jack. She needed to stop getting so immersed in other people's lives. Hadn't Seth stated last night that he was looking for a certain kind of woman to raise his son? His list of qualifications had flashed across her mind like a giant billboard, reminding her that she didn't meet any of them. His bullet points hadn't included a criminal past, a childhood of abuse and a close relative in prison. She had to get a grip on her emotions and keep the cold facts of reality at the forefront of her mind. She had no future with Seth.

But how could she do that when she cared so much for both of them?

Seth shoved his phone into his shirt pocket and scraped his hands through his hair. If he didn't know better he'd think the universe was against him. But he knew the Lord had His hand on his life and it would eventually work out. He also understood that the Lord knew the long-term scope of his existence, and that meant that there was no guarantee Jack would end up with him.

He glanced over his shoulder and saw Carrie and Jack walking hand in hand toward him. The little boy's face was covered in a huge smile, and he looked up with adoring eyes at Carrie. She in turn gazed upon him with such love and affection his heart swelled with warmth. Carrie was an amazing woman. But they'd agreed to be friends only. Neither of them was in the market for anything more, though he couldn't deny that he was beginning to think of more than friendship with his lovely neighbor.

Carrie's blue eyes were filled with worry when she stopped in front of him. He was glad she was here with him. He needed her support right now.

"Is everything okay?"

He couldn't find the words yet, so he scooped up Jack and held him close. "How about a few more trips down the slide before we go home?" Jack squealed in delight. Seth set him down and he dashed off full speed toward the playground.

"Seth?"

He took her hand, needing the contact, then started toward the playground equipment to watch Jack. He stopped at the bay of swings and sat in one. Carrie took the swing beside him.

"What happened? You're scaring me. Is it about Jack?"

"That was the lab calling. They misplaced the DNA test. We'll have to take a new one. That means another two, maybe three, weeks until we get the results."

Carrie reached over and took his hand. "Oh, Seth, I'm so sorry. I was hoping this would be settled in a few days."

He rubbed his thumb across her hand. "Me, too. I'd convinced myself that the results would prove Jack was mine. I was ready to set up a college fund. Dumb, huh?"

"No, not at all. I know you want an answer. It's awful living in limbo with all these unanswered questions."

"That's why I'm glad I have you. I couldn't have done this alone."

"Yes, you could. Your family would have helped."

He nodded. "True, but it wouldn't have been the same." Sighing, he asked, "Would you mind if we stopped by the doctor's office on the way home? The sooner I get this test sent out, the better."

"Of course not."

Seth gave her hand a squeeze before letting go and standing. Knowing she was on his side made everything so much easier. "Jack. Time to go, buddy."

Seth moved toward the little boy, smiling at the frown on his face. "I don't think he's ready to leave the park." When Carrie didn't respond, he turned and saw her staring into the distance, one hand clutching the swing chain. She looked terrified. Her usually rosy cheeks were pale and drawn, and her eyes wide.

"Carrie?" His concern grew when she continued to stand like a statue. He could see her rapid breathing from where he stood. "Carrie." She blinked and looked at him, but it took a moment for her to focus. He touched her shoulder and she flinched. "What's wrong? Are you sick?" He glanced over his shoulder in the direction she'd been staring, but didn't see anything out of the ordinary. "Talk to me."

She inhaled a shaky breath and shook her head.

"Nothing. Really. I thought I saw…" She shook her head again. "It's nothing." She smiled and stepped past him. "Jack, sweetie, let's go. We can come back another day."

Seth kept a close eye on Carrie as they drove home. She was withdrawn and tense. He wanted to take her home and see if he could find out what was bothering her, but he needed to get to the doctor's office to have the DNA test taken. Thankfully, it only took a few minutes and they were on their way home again.

"So you want to tell me what really happened back there in the park?"

It took her a long time to reply. "I thought I saw someone. But it's impossible. He's…far away."

Seth pulled his truck to a stop under the carport behind his house and got out. After letting Jack out, he opened Carrie's door. "Let's have a glass of iced tea and talk. I promised sandwiches for lunch, remember?"

Reluctantly she agreed. Seth gave her time to gather her thoughts as they worked side by side preparing ham and cheese sandwiches. He sliced the first one in half crosswise.

"I thought I saw my brother, Neil."

"You said that was impossible. Why?"

"He's in prison."

Not what he'd expected. "Could he have been released?"

"I don't know. He wasn't up for parole until next month."

"I can look into it if you want me to."

"No! Please. I don't want to know anything about him. It wasn't him today. I was wrong."

Her reaction alarmed him. She was shaking and pale, and she never raised her voice to anyone. A brother who was a criminal might explain a lot about Carrie's history. "Is he the one who put you in the closet?" The truth was written in her pain-filled eyes. "And is he the reason you changed your name?"

"How did you know about that? How many other things do you know?" She covered her face with her hands. "This can't be happening. Not now."

"It's all right. I won't tell anyone, and the other person has been warned to keep that information to himself."

"How can you be sure?"

"Because otherwise he'll have to answer to me."

Carrie wiped her hands on the dish towel and picked up her purse. "I need to go home. I'm not hungry. Thanks for your help today."

"Carrie, don't go. I want to understand. I want to help."

"You can't. No one can. And I don't want you to understand."

Seth spent much of the afternoon and evening trying to sort out Carrie's reaction and sift through the pieces of information she'd shared since they met. He'd tried to find out about a Neil Fletcher, but came up empty. Without knowing Carrie's birth name, he was stumped. He had the means to find out, but he wasn't going to invade her privacy. Not until there was a reason beyond his own curiosity.

He wanted her to trust him enough to share her past. All of it. Obviously he'd have to give her a lot more time.

In the meantime, he'd keep a close watch on her. He'd never forgive himself if something happened to her.

Carrie sat on the sofa Wednesday evening while Jack stretched out on the floor watching the movie about cars again and fiddling with one of the small pocket-size cars she'd bought him recently. The others were stuffed securely in his pockets.

Things had settled into their normal pattern. Seth was back on his midday schedule, which gave her plenty of time with Jack after work until Seth picked him up and they had dinner together. She'd feared things would change between them after she'd admitted changing her name, but they hadn't. If anything, Seth had been even more protective. A gesture that left her with mixed emotions. While she found his extra concern sweet, she worried his curiosity would lead him to dig into her past.

Seth had been a big help this week, making arrangements for the shuttle service, picking up orders around town and taking over the arrangements for getting Vern Bailey's vintage plane to the park the morning of the picnic.

Without him, organizing this picnic would have been much harder. His connections around town had proved to be a blessing, and she'd grown a bit envious. Seth had roots, bonds that linked him not only to the people living in Dover now but those who'd come before. He knew how various people were related. He remembered when so-and-so owned a store and who had bought it. Dover was a deep thread through his life. For all his trying to get away, he seemed woven into the fabric of this little town. She wondered if he appreciated how special that was. She would give anything to have a family. Grandparents, cousins, aunts and uncles. Her gaze drifted to Jack as he played. God willing, he would be surrounded by family the rest of his life and be protected by a strong, loving father.

A glance at the clock reminded her Seth would be here soon and she needed to get his meal ready. Tonight she had prepared Jack's favorite—spaghetti. The volume of the movie increased, making her smile. Jack had found the remote. He liked to hear his favorite car chase as loud as he could.

A bubble of anticipation zinged through her the moment the tapping sounded on the back door. She'd told Seth repeatedly that he could come in without knocking, but he'd said it was the gentlemanly thing to do and his mother would scold him if she found out.

A teasing comment was on her lips as she opened the door. But it wasn't Seth who stood there. The man at her door was the one person she'd hoped to never see again.

Her brother, Neil.

She started to shut the door, but he shouldered inside. "Hey, baby sis."

She held her ground, refusing to move enough to allow him farther into the room. "What are you doing here? You're supposed to be in prison."

"They let me out early on good behavior."

"You're not welcome here."

"Aren't you glad to see me? It's been a long time. I had a little trouble tracking you down." He pointed a finger at her. "You changed your name. That wasn't very nice. Are you ashamed of your big brother? You should have chosen something other than mom's maiden name."

"Neil, you need to leave. Now." Fear tightened her throat, making it hard to breathe. She'd never been strong enough to refuse his demands. He'd always been able to control her with the threat of abandonment. But not today. Her greater fear now was for Jack. She couldn't let Neil know the little boy was here. For once she was grateful for the volume of the television.

Silently she prayed for strength to stand up to her brother and to protect little Jack. "Leave. We have nothing to say to each other." She stepped in front of him, heart pounding but refusing to show fear.

"Sure thing, sis. All I need is a few bucks to get out of the country. Five grand would do it."

"Are you kidding? I don't have that kind of money." He took a step closer, his smoker's breath assaulting her nose, his hard blue eyes devoid of any kindness above his cruel smirk.

"You're lying. You have a house and a great job. You can swing it."

"I rent this place and my money is tied up in a 401(k), which means I can't get to it."

He cocked his head and glared. "Then I'll take whatever you got. You owe me. We're blood."

She fought to keep her voice low and not give any hint of the child in the next room. She didn't want to think what her brother might do to get what he wanted. "I don't owe you anything. I'm done doing what you tell me."

Carrie stared him down, her mind repeating the prayer for strength. The sound of an approaching car drew Neil's attention. He glanced over his shoulder at the headlights in the alley. He backed out the door. "I'll be back."

"Don't bother. I won't help you. Ever."

"We'll see about that."

Neil disappeared into the dark and Carrie locked the door, set the dead bolt and leaned against the door, fighting her racing heart. "Thank you, Lord. You are my strength." The Lord had answered her prayer. He'd given her the strength to confront Neil and hold her ground.

A knock sounded on the door and she let out a yelp. But this time the face on the other side was Seth. Relief weakened her knees. She yanked open the door, wanting desperately to throw herself into his arms but managing to restrain herself. If she did there'd be questions. Too many she couldn't answer. "Hey. We've been waiting for you."

His gaze told her he knew something was wrong. "Everything all right?"

She nodded. "Yes." Quickly she moved to the counter, trying to hide the shaking in her hands. She should tell him about Neil. He was a cop. He could make sure her brother didn't come around again. But she didn't want her past or her brother touching anything in her new life. Telling Seth would get him involved. It would be safer if she handled it herself.

She spoke over her shoulder as she stirred the reheated meal. "Jack's watching the car movie again and supper is ready."

Secretly she'd hoped he would stay awhile. Seth's presence in her home was like a protective shield. Silly. She could take care of herself, and had most of her life. But she couldn't deny having Seth at her side gave her added courage, knowing he would back her up.

She heard Seth speak to his son and the loud squeal of delight from the little boy.

"Pop. You're home. I missed you."

Seth hugged him tight. "I missed you, too."

By the time they sat down to supper, she was feeling calmer and in control. Seth, however, seemed tired and preoccupied, and he gathered Jack up as soon as he finished eating. "Oh, this is my long weekend, and I'll be working days. Mom's going to keep Jack, so you'll have your weekend to yourself."

"I don't mind watching him for you."

"I know, but you deserve some time off." He stopped in the doorway and turned around. "I know something is bothering you. I can see it in your eyes. If you need me, you know you can call anytime. Even if it's only to talk."

"I know. That means a lot."

She watched them go, then locked up again, wishing she could confide in Seth. He was the one person who could help protect her from Neil, but she couldn't tell him the whole story. That would mean admitting she was a criminal, and he'd already been hurt deeply by one woman with a record. Telling him was the right thing to do, but it would cost her his friendship and her time with Jack. Apparently, she had exhausted her strength in standing up to Neil, because she had none when it came to doing the right thing where Seth and Jack were concerned.

Chapter Nine

Carrie made her way down the hallway of the church toward her office. It had been two days since Neil had shown up at her house, with no further contact. She'd prayed fervently that he'd moved on. A part of her knew that was unlikely, but it had allowed her to sleep last night.

She'd talked to Mavis several times and had learned that Neil's parole hearing had been moved up and he'd been released early. Mavis had offered to come to Dover and stay with her, but Carrie had refused. Her friend had also encouraged her to tell the police. Carrie knew she would have to tell Seth eventually, but she'd already told Seth too much about her past. Telling him about Neil would mean she'd have to tell him everything.

Pastor Jim passed her in the hall as she neared her office and Gloria Warner, the church secretary, waved as she pushed open her door. Carrie set her purse on the small table behind her desk and sat down. She had a lot to do today, which was why she'd come in early.

Her gaze came to rest on the desktop and she frowned. Something wasn't right. Her laptop. It was gone. She glanced around. It wasn't on the small overstuffed chair or the lamp table. Had she taken it home and forgotten? Unlikely.

"No! No!"

Carrie hurried out into the hall when she heard Gloria shout. Pastor Jim was hurrying toward her, as well.

"Pastor. My laptop is gone. I've looked everywhere."

Carrie nodded. "Mine, too."

Pastor Jim sighed. "And mine."

Gloria looked to the pastor for guidance. "What should we do?"

"Call the police. Don't touch anything and we'll let them take it from here."

Reluctant to go back into her office, Carrie paced the hallway as they waited. Why the laptops? They were old and not worth much, and the information on them held value only for the church.

She glanced up when the back door opened, relieved to see Seth walk in. She smiled but he didn't return it. His attitude was stern and professional. She'd never seen him on duty. This must be how he looked to the people he arrested. She had to admit he was an imposing sight.

He stopped in front of Pastor Jim. "We've received an anonymous tip about your missing laptops."

"Already? We only discovered it a half hour ago."

"The call came in just a few minutes ago." Seth faced Carrie. "Miss Fletcher, would you please open the trunk of your car."

Miss Fletcher? Why was he so formal? Her heart

pounded in her ears. She knew with certainty that her past had finally caught up with her, but what did he think she'd done?

The door opened again and Phil Hagen walked in. He spoke quietly to Seth, then stepped back, resting his hands on his duty belt. Carrie's blood chilled. The expression on Seth's face was grim and he looked pale. Something was very wrong.

"The trunk, please."

Carrie retrieved her keys and started toward the back door, the two officers following close behind. She pushed the button on the key fob and waited while Seth looked into her trunk.

She was vaguely aware of Pastor Jim and Gloria coming to her side. Seth glanced into her trunk and she saw his shoulders sag.

"Pastor, are these the missing computers?"

Jim hurried forward, exhaling a heavy sigh before glancing at Carrie. "Yes."

She was horrified to see the three laptops in her trunk.

Seth's expression was unemotional, but his eyes were filled with regret.

Carrie's mind reeled. "I didn't take those. Why would I? You have to believe me."

Pastor Jim slipped an arm around her shoulders. "Of course you didn't. There has to be some explanation."

Gloria came to her side. "Carrie would never steal anything. Certainly not three old computers."

Carrie's insides twisted into a scalding knot. Her body was on fire. But she *had* stolen. Not this time, but in the past. She looked at Seth, who avoided meeting her gaze. "I didn't do this." Her knees suddenly gave way and she sagged against Pastor Jim.

"I'm sure this is just a misunderstanding."

"Maybe, but I still have to take her to the station for questioning."

Seth's voice sounded so cold and hard.

Carrie's stomach flipped over. Her insides burned and her skin felt hot and cold. Neil was behind this. She didn't know how he'd pulled it off, but it was something he would do. He wanted to discredit her so she'd help him get away.

Seth looked at her for the first time and she saw the pain in his eyes. It gave her a small measure of comfort. He didn't want to do this, but he would. He would always do his duty.

He pulled the handcuffs from his belt.

Carrie spun and buried her head in Pastor Jim's shoulder. "Pastor, please. I didn't do this."

"I know. Don't worry, we'll get it all sorted out."

Carrie's mind shut down, and she curled inward to a place she hadn't been in a long time. Survival mode. Don't think. Don't feel. Just one step in front of the other. Do what had to be done, and pray.

"Watch your head."

The words, spoken in Seth's deep slightly raspy voice, sliced through to her core. Her life was unraveling like a kitten pulling on a strand of a sweater and there was nothing she could do to stop it.

They rode in silence to the police station. Carrie was

grateful that Seth didn't speak. There was nothing she could say, no way she could explain.

When Seth parked the cruiser, he looked at her through the rearview mirror. "I'm sorry, Carrie. I'll get to the bottom of this. I promise."

She closed her eyes and turned away. It was only a matter of time now. Her past would be discovered, and then the whole town would know.

Seth paced along the front sidewalk of the police station, waiting for his mother to arrive. A giant jackhammer pounded inside his skull, and his heart beat so violently inside his chest that his ribs ached. He'd handed Carrie over to be questioned and immediately called his mom and the family attorney.

Tension coiled tightly in his gut, building until he wanted to smash something. Anything to untangle his confusion. He'd been convinced the whole anonymous call was a hoax, and he'd gone to the church to prove it. Then Phil had whispered in his ear that he'd checked and discovered Carrie had a sealed juvenile record. The caller said she'd served time for theft. Even if it were true, Seth knew firsthand how easy it was for kids to get into trouble. Carrie had admitted she grew up in a rough neighborhood. Her record could be for something minor.

He refused to believe Carrie was guilty. The whole thing smelled like a setup. But who would want to discredit Carrie? Everyone loved her. She was warm and caring and friendly.

Tiff had been likable, too. It's how she'd wormed her

way into people's confidence, then tricked them out of their money. And he'd been a dumb, naive kid from small-town Mississippi, too green to understand the real world and how people could use others without regard.

He'd vowed to be more cautious in his relationships. He'd believed he'd be more attuned to the wrong type of woman the next time, but Carrie had slipped under his radar and under his skin.

Was Carrie using him? Was he still a naive idiot?

There was no way he could put Carrie in the same category as Tiff. His former wife had been a self-absorbed pleasure seeker, always looking for a good time and money to spend. Carrie rarely thought of herself. Her motives were always focused on others. There had to be an explanation for her juvenile record and this attack on her integrity.

She was innocent. He refused to accept any other outcome. He'd called his mother and the family attorney to handle the situation. Next, he'd look into Carrie's brother, Neil. His gut was telling him he was behind this. No one else in Dover would have a reason to tag Carrie as a thief.

More than that, he didn't want to believe Carrie was guilty. She was his friend, a good friend. He rubbed his eyes. Who was he kidding? He was in love with Carrie. He wasn't sure when it had happened. Maybe when they'd sat on the kid swings at the park and she'd encouraged him. Maybe it was seeing the love in her eyes for Jack, or the moment when the lights went out and he'd held her in his arms and nearly kissed her. Whenever it was, it had snuck up on him.

What a mess his life was. He was in love with a woman who didn't want a relationship, and who might be a thief. He had a little boy in his life whom he dearly loved but might not be his. His heart was tangled up with them both, and there was a very good chance that he could lose them both. But first he had to take care of Carrie and somehow keep his feelings hidden while he did it.

The next half hour of Carrie's life passed in a blur. Old memories from her youth scorched her mind. She looked around the small room where they'd taken her after her arrival at the police station. A female officer had questioned her. Since then she'd seen no one. She clasped her hands on the scarred tabletop, and her gaze landed on her wrists. Seth had pulled out his handcuffs but hadn't put them on her. He hadn't read her her Miranda rights or anything. Was that a good thing or not?

Her mind was only now starting to digest what had happened. Her heart ached as if someone had reached in and torn it from her body. *You are my strength.* The verse didn't bring the comfort she'd expected. Why had the Lord let this happen? Why had Neil invaded her life again? How had he even found her?

What did Seth think about her now? He'd never speak to her again, and watching Jack was out of the question. She must be in shock or something because she hadn't even cried. The tears would form behind her eyes and then never fall. Closing her eyes, she prayed again, looking for comfort but finding only despair.

"Carrie, honey."

She looked up to find Francie Montgomery coming into the room. The friendly face gave her a flicker of comfort, but it was instantly replaced with a wave of shame and humiliation.

"Carrie. It's okay, we've come to take you home. This is our attorney, Blake Prescott. He's arranged for your release."

Carrie stole a glance at the man beside Francie. He was a tall, dark-haired man with keen eyes and a face made for a magazine ad. She looked back at Seth's mother. Was she really going home? She wanted to hide in her little house, hold Leo and give herself over to the grief. She'd lost everything today.

Suddenly she was wrapped in a warm embrace. Francie patted her back.

"It'll be all right, Carrie. Blake is going to handle everything. You don't have to worry about a thing."

"The church doesn't want to press charges so you're free to go, Miss Fletcher." Prescott handed her his business card. "If the authorities want to talk to you again or if you have any questions, call me, day or night."

She nodded. Would the police come after her again? Francie led her out into the hall and Carrie became aware of all the eyes watching her. She lowered her gaze. If only she could melt into the floor. Could this get any more humiliating? Francie guided her through the building and out to her car. She found herself looking for Seth as they walked through the station, and at the same time hoping she would not see him.

The sight of her little cottage as they pulled up filled her with relief. Leo greeted her happily as they stepped into the living room. She picked him up and held him close to her neck, then faced Mrs. Montgomery. "I don't know how to thank you. I'm sorry I let you down."

"Honey, you haven't let anyone down. No one believes for a moment that you took those computers. It's absurd."

Carrie shook her head, tears forming again in her eyes. "No. This will change everything. I'll lose my job and I'll have to move again. I really wanted Dover to be my forever home. But after this, everyone will hate me." Especially Seth.

"I know you feel like that now, but it's not true. It'll be a hot topic for a few days, but it'll pass. You have more friends here than you know. Once the truth comes out, it'll all fade away."

Carrie wished that were true. "No. It'll be like a tag at the end of my name. People will look at me and say, 'That's Carrie Fletcher. She has a record, you know. Bless her heart.'"

The truth coming out wouldn't change anything. Everyone would know she was a thief and believe that she had schemed to rob the church. This was one situation where the truth wouldn't set her free. It would only send her back to a prison—of shame.

"Are you going to be all right here alone? I can stay if you'd like."

"No, thank you. That's very kind, but I need time to process things."

"I understand. Oh, we'll get your car to you. And, please, if you need anything call me. I'm always here to help."

The moment the door closed behind Seth's mother, the house went still as a tomb. For now it was what she wanted. No people, no noise, nothing but silence. Cradling Leo, she curled up on the sofa and closed her eyes, letting the pain of the day take over. The knock on the door forced her eyes open.

"Carrie. It's me, Seth."

No. Not Seth. She wasn't ready to face him yet. Why was he here? Holding Leo close, quietly she rose, made her way to the dining room and stood in the corner. If he peeked in the front window or the back door, he couldn't see her in this spot.

He pounded on the door. "Carrie, I know you're in there. Please let me in."

If she ignored him long enough, he'd go away. Wouldn't he?

"Carrie, honey. We need to talk."

Talking was the last thing she wanted to do.

"Okay, I'll give you some time, but I'll be back, and I'll pick the lock if I have to."

There was that protective streak of his again. Doing what he had to for those he cared about. Though she doubted he cared as much now as he might have this morning.

Thankfully, she heard him stepping off the porch. Cautiously she peered out the window in time to see his cruiser disappear down the street. And probably out of her life forever.

Seth's mom hurried toward him and wrapped him in a hug the moment he stepped inside her house.

"How's Carrie? Did you talk to her?"

"She wouldn't let me in. I'm going to try again later."

"Good, because she needs you. This has been a terrible shock to her. Poor thing. I hope you get the scoundrel who did this."

"I will. I think it was her brother."

"Why would he want to frame her like that?"

Seth sank into a chair at the breakfast table, clasping his hands in front of his chin. "Not sure. She's hinted that her childhood was difficult, and that her brother locked her in a closet. She's been afraid of the dark ever since. She sleeps with all the lights on."

"That sweet woman doesn't deserve any of this."

When he didn't comment, his mother took a closer look. "What aren't you telling me?"

"Carrie does have a juvenile record. The caller said it was for theft, but I don't know the details since the file is sealed."

"And that bothers you? Why?"

Seth searched for a place to start. "My ex-wife, Tiff. She was a crook, Mom. She tricked people out of their money, scammed them out of their identity. I fell for her hard, and she wasn't what I thought."

"And you think you've done the same thing with Carrie?"

"I have. I would have staked my life on her being a decent law-abiding citizen, and now I found out she's a thief. I seem to always pick the wrong women."

"Okay. Stop right there. I'm sure it was shock, but you're forgetting that record is from her childhood. It could be for anything. But it doesn't matter. What does is who she is now, today."

"I don't know…"

"Have you told her about your less-than-noble past? You're not in a position to look down on anyone else's transgressions, son."

"I've told her most of it."

"Then she could have the same reaction to your sins as you're having to hers."

The question hit him hard. He was being harsh and judgmental. To the woman he'd claimed to love.

His mom crossed her arms over her chest. "How long did it take you to figure out the woman you married was the wrong one? That she wasn't what you thought?"

He shrugged. "A couple weeks."

"And how long have you known Carrie?"

"A month or so." Her point wasn't lost on him. He'd known Carrie long enough to see she was all she appeared to be. He knew that in his heart, but he'd been burned once before.

"Son, you may not know it yet, but you're in love with Carrie, and I for one am delighted. She makes you happy, you smile more and she complements your more serious nature. And she loves Jack. She's a woman of faith. Aren't those things more important than whether she made a mistake in the past?"

Seth ran a hand through his hair. Everything his mother said was true, but after his big mistake with Tiff, how could he trust himself to choose the right woman?

His mom laid her hand on his. "You could have a

good future with Carrie, maybe even build a home on your land and be close to me."

Seth frowned. "I don't have any land, remember? Another part of my life I squandered away."

"Well, actually that was my money you lived off in Vegas."

"What are you talking about?"

She exhaled a deep sigh. "Your father and I knew you'd come to your senses eventually, and we knew you'd regret selling your inheritance. So, I took out a loan on the real estate business and we told you it was from the sale of your property."

Seth leaned back in his chair, trying to absorb what she was telling him. "Mom, I had no idea. I don't know what to say."

"Nothing. It's what parents do for their children."

He grasped his mother's hand. "Mom. I'll pay you back. Every cent plus interest."

"I don't want your money, sweetheart. Just promise me you'll build a home on that land someday and be happy. Hopefully with Carrie."

Seth was back. Carrie looked out her front window as a cruiser pulled up at the curb and Seth got out. Why couldn't he just leave well enough alone? Hadn't the day been painful enough?

He knocked on the door. She stood still and hoped he'd go away like he had earlier.

"Carrie, I'm not leaving, so you might as well let me in."

She ran her hands through her hair. The sooner she

got this over with, the sooner she could move on. She opened the door, noticing Seth was out of uniform. He wore jeans and a dark T-shirt with a small Dover Police logo on the front. The shirt emphasized the breadth of his chest and the well-developed biceps that strained the fabric. He looked so handsome, and she wanted to bury her head in his chest and feel the sense of security she'd known there. But she couldn't.

"Are you going to leave that police car parked in front of my house all night? You might as well tell everyone a criminal lives here." Her words came out harsher than she'd intended.

"No. It's telling everyone you're protected. I want anyone who might drive by here to know you're being watched."

"You mean like Neil?" She tried to meet his penetrating gaze, but only managed a flicker of connection before shame rushed through her again. He took a step toward her, and she spun around and headed for the kitchen. She couldn't face him. "I need to let Leo in."

"You can't put this off forever, Carrie."

Being alone with Seth was the last thing she wanted right now. But postponing this conversation wouldn't help, either. She wanted this done. Finished. Then she could start putting her life back together. Leo scratched at the door and she let him in, her nerves on edge as she waited for Seth to start demanding answers.

"Carrie. Look at me."

She shook her head, humiliating tears spilling from her eyes. Why did they come now when she wanted to look strong and confident for Seth?

Gentle hands grasped her shoulders and pulled her around. She opened her eyes, but kept them focused on the center of his chest. She concentrated on the steady rise and fall of his muscular torso. He pulled her close, lifting her chin with his hand and forcing her to meet his gaze. Once she looked into his eyes she was lost.

"Carrie, I'm so sorry. Can you ever forgive me for what I did?"

Forgive him? No, she needed to ask for his forgiveness. "It wasn't your fault."

With one gentle tug he wrapped her in his arms, cradling her head in his palm. "I can't imagine how scared you were. I wanted to hold you, not take you into custody. I knew you were innocent, but I don't understand why someone would want to accuse you and set you up like that."

The comfort she found in his arms was sweeter than anything she'd ever known. Seth made her feel protected, treasured and loved. But she had to tell him the whole truth now, and then he wouldn't want to comfort her—he'd want to distance himself.

"I know who." She pushed away, searching for breathing room. "My brother, Neil."

"Your brother? Why would he do that?"

"He came by the other night wanting money to leave the country. I turned him down."

"That's what was bothering you that night. Why didn't you tell me? I could have done something."

"I didn't want you to know about…him." She walked into the living room. Seth followed close behind.

"So you think Neil set you up to force you to help him? Why?"

"I think he's angry that I created a new life for myself and he wants to ruin it. He's always blamed everyone else for his failures."

"Is your brother the only one who knew about your record?"

She nodded, a rush of heat filling her neck. "And my friend Mavis, of course."

"Then he's probably the one who told us to look for your file under your real name. Carrie Lynn Overton."

Carrie's blood turned to ice. "You read my file?" Carrie sank onto the sofa, stunned. "I thought it would be sealed forever and no one would ever know. But I always feared it would come out eventually. Now it has."

Seth joined her on the sofa. "No one opened your file. That would take a court order. But I would like to know what happened. Help me understand what's going on."

No need to keep the truth from him any longer. She'd lost everything she cared about. All she could do now was come clean and let the Lord sort it all out. "Neil was my guardian after our dad abandoned us. But he wasn't much more than a kid himself. He tried his best to support us but it was hard. He got in with a bad crowd and started robbing to put food on the table. Even that wasn't enough, so he got me involved, too. He told me if I didn't steal he'd leave me, too, and I'd be all alone. I was only fourteen. I couldn't work, didn't have an education. I was terrified of being left alone. So I did what he told me. Mainly I acted as a distraction while he and his friends did the stealing. I'd go in first and either ask for help or break something, then they would come in and rob the place. Sometimes I shoplifted things. One night we went to a small grocery store, only this time Neil had a gun. I'd never seen him with one before. I was supposed to distract them by stealing something, only it all went wrong and the store manager was shot and we were all caught. I had merchandise in my hand, so I was sentenced to a year in juvenile detention. Neil got fifteen years in prison."

"Is that when you changed your name?"

"Not right away. I met a woman in detention who was teaching a Bible study. She befriended me, got me an attorney who managed to have me released early and Mavis took me home to live with her. She helped me with my GED and college entrance, and suggested I change my name. New name. New life."

She looked at Seth and could see the shock and disappointment in his eyes. What else had she expected? "So you see, I *am* a thief. I didn't take the laptops, but I am a criminal."

"You were just a kid trying to survive."

She shook her head. "I'm no better than Jack's mother."

"No. You're nothing like Jack's mom. I don't care about your past. It's done. You've paid for your mistake."

"I'll have to quit my job and leave Dover. No one will want me around anymore. I'll have to find someone to take over the picnic."

"You can't leave Dover. What would Jack and I do without you?"

The truth must have not sunk in with him yet. He didn't understand. "Seth."

"Carrie, I won't let anything happen to you. I promise. You mean a great deal to me. I promise I'll keep you safe."

He tilted her chin upward. The look in his eyes held so much tenderness she wanted to look away, but it was impossible. Their gazes meshed.

She went into his arms as if she belonged there. He kissed her slowly, tenderly at first, but then he deepened the kiss. She returned it with all the emotion she'd been holding in check and knew he was feeling the same. There was no denying the way they felt about each other.

He pulled away, whispered her name, then recaptured her mouth again.

She floated on the sweet connection between them, willing to remain in his arms for the rest of her life. He raised his head, then tugged her close. She knew she should send him home, but all she wanted was to make this moment last as long as it could.

She'd deal with reality tomorrow.

"We'll get him, Carrie. I'll make sure he doesn't come near you ever again."

Monday morning dawned bright, warm and sunny. A direct contrast to her life. Since Seth had left her home Friday night, she'd hidden herself inside. She had been grateful he was on duty all weekend. It kept him from dropping in. She didn't want him to see her in this condition. She'd barely slept, and eating was out of the question with her stomach tied in a permanent knot. Her dreams had been filled with images of Seth and of the kiss they'd shared. But they'd all ended with him leaving her alone on a cliff with dark clouds overhead. The dreams were like salt in a wound because in the middle of this mess she'd realized that she was dangerously close to being in love with Seth Montgomery. She'd tried her hardest to protect her heart, but her efforts had been wasted. She was lost.

Cradling her coffee cup in her hand, she curled up on the sofa and stared out the front window. She wanted to sit on her porch swing, but that would expose her to the world and she wasn't ready for that. Her emotions were so muddled she couldn't begin to sort them out. One minute she was full of joy remembering Seth's kiss, and her newfound love would bring a smile to her face. Then next she would face the truth that she would have to leave Dover. She'd already started writing her resignation.

Her other big concern was the anniversary picnic. Someone had to step in and complete the details. It was only a week away. Too many people were counting on that celebration. But no matter who she thought of, no one had the knowledge to finish the arrangements.

A knock on the front door startled her. She didn't want to see anyone. Ever again. She rose and looked through the peephole. Pastor Jim. A wave of guilt swelled. She hadn't gone into work this morning. She hadn't even called in sick. She opened the door.

"Good morning. How are you doing today?"

She forced a smile and motioned him inside. Maybe a minister was exactly what she needed.

He patted her shoulder, glancing at her open Bible as he passed the end table. "Searching for a verse that will make it all better?"

"I suppose."

"I've done that. You might have more success in *Proverbs* or *Psalms*." He positioned himself in the armchair and crossed his legs. "I wanted to know when you'll be coming back to work."

"I'm not. I mean, I didn't think you'd want me back after…"

"Of *course* we want you back. Carrie, you are an important part of our staff. In fact—" he pulled an envelope from his jacket "—they sent this to you."

She slipped the card out and smiled at the pretty flowers and birds on the front under the words *Thinking of You*. Inside were scribbled messages of encouragement from every staff member and all the committee heads. She couldn't believe it. Tears blurred her vision. "They want me back?"

"Yes. Besides, no one else in the church can keep that picnic on track. You are some kind of superwoman. It's only a week away, you know."

"I want to come back. But I can't."

"I think you can. It won't be easy, but you can do it. I have faith in you."

A firm knock on her door drew her to her feet. She opened the door and was shocked to see Lorna Gathers holding a casserole dish. Lorna was infamous for her sour attitude and constant disapproval of everything. "Hello, Miss Lorna."

She shoved the dish toward her. "It's tuna. You need to come back to work." She shifted her weight as if uncomfortable. "We can't hold this picnic without you." She pivoted and started to step off the porch, then stopped and looked over her shoulder. "Don't break my dish."

Pastor Jim glanced beyond Carrie's shoulder. "What were you saying about people hating you? That's the first time Lorna has brought anyone food."

Carrie looked at the dish in her hands. "That was very sweet."

Jim patted her shoulder. "I'll leave you. But I hope when I arrive at church tomorrow morning you'll be in your office hard at work. Don't forget, we all have things in our past we regret. But once we've confessed and obtained forgiveness from the Lord, it's over. Sometimes the hard part is learning how to forgive ourselves."

After saying a prayer and promising to think about returning to work the next day, Jim left and Carrie thumbed to *Psalms* in her Bible. The pastor was right. She did have a hard time forgiving her past. Her fears had created the mess she was in now. But she'd been through more difficult situations and she'd learned those were the times when the Lord was sculpting her into something better, shaving off the spurs, chipping away the crusty spots so she could see and understand more clearly. She'd come to think of them as spiritual root canals—kill the infection, removed the dead parts, then replace it with a solid new tooth that would last forever.

But what was He trying to teach her now? Not to love? To return her focus to her goal to be a social worker? She had no idea, but she had a lot to think about. Her gaze landed on the card lying on her coffee table. Picking it up, she reread the names and the well-wishes.

Did they really want her back? The idea should have terrified her, but, instead, a sense of peace settled deep inside. Maybe it was time to step out in faith and see what the Lord had in store.

Chapter Ten

Seth held Jack in his arms as he knocked on the Carrie's front door Monday evening. The little guy hadn't seen her in days, since the laptop incident. Seth had given her the whole weekend to find her footing again, but she was still holed up in her house, not taking calls, not going out, and Pastor Jim said she hadn't come to work today. That was not like Carrie.

Jack leaned forward and rapped his little knuckles on the door. "Maybe she didn't hear you, Pop."

Seth smiled. "Maybe not."

"Did she go away? Will she come back again? I miss her and Leo."

"I miss her, too. Miss Carrie hasn't been feeling well, but she'll get better." He needed to see her, to talk to her. After the kiss they'd shared, his emotions had been on a roller coaster. He needed to know where they stood. Kissing Carrie had caused a seismic shift in his thinking. Everything had changed between them and he needed to talk to her about it.

"Did she go to the doctor and get a shot?"

If only emotional distress was so easily healed. "I don't know. We'll have to ask her." He had raised his fist to knock again when suddenly the door opened. Her gaze collided with his, then quickly slid to Jack, and a sweet smile brightened her face. That was the sunshine girl he'd fallen in love with.

"Jack wanted to come see you." Jack wiggled in his grasp, waving at Carrie. She reached for him and he lunged into her arms, hugging her neck.

"I love you, Miss Carrie." He squeezed tight and emitted a little grunt to emphasize the hug.

"I love you, too, Jack." She carried him inside, setting him down when Leo came racing from the other room. The pair hugged and wrestled with happiness.

"Looks like Leo missed Jack as much as he missed that fur ball."

"Probably more than he missed me."

Seth let his gaze skim over her face, from the short wavy blond hair that gave her a girlish look to her creamy skin and the little throbbing pulse in her neck. "I missed you, too."

She met his eyes and his breath caught in his throat. She was beautiful inside and out, and he couldn't imagine a day in his life without her.

"I missed you…both."

He took her hand and pulled her down beside him on the couch. Jack went straight to the small box of toys she'd collected since he'd come into her life. "How are you, Carrie? I was getting worried. You wouldn't take my calls, you'd locked yourself in the house and you didn't go to work this morning. Pastor Jim said you might not go back to work."

She cast her eyes down. "I'm not ready to face anyone yet."

"You can't stay in hiding forever. And they aren't just anyone. They're your friends. I can't tell you how many times I get asked about you during the day."

Carrie rolled her eyes. "How's the thief doing today and when is she leaving town?"

"No. Just the opposite. They all know you were framed. No one thinks you took those laptops."

Carrie pulled her hand from his. "Any news on Neil? Is he still here in town?"

"We're still tracking him down. He showed up in Sawyer's Bend a few days ago and someone reported he was in Natchez, but we can't confirm either. We have established he has a partner."

Carried rubbed her eyes. "So there are two men I need to worry about now?"

"You don't need to worry. I'm right next door and I've been keeping an eye on you."

"Thanks, but I hate to be so much trouble."

"No trouble. I like watching out for you. I want to keep you safe." He leaned forward and kissed her. She ended it, pushing him away.

"You shouldn't get involved with me."

"Too late."

"I'm serious. I don't know what my brother will do next. What if he shows up at the church? I could be putting others in danger."

"If that's what you're worried about, I'll take you to and from work every day."

"No. That's not necessary."

"What about the picnic? Who's going to finish all the preparations for that?"

She wrung her hands together. "I don't know. I can't find anyone."

"That's because you're the only one who can pull all this together. I know you—you won't let those people down. It's not who you are."

"I don't want to, but what if Neil shows up again?"

"Then I'll deal with him. You let me handle that. And let me help with the picnic, too. Let me do the things you're reluctant to tackle. But, Carrie, I know you don't want to let anyone else manage the picnic."

Her cell phone rang and she shifted to pick it up. Tears welled up in her blue eyes. She nodded, then muttered a soft thank-you before hanging up. The tears rolled down her cheeks and he wrapped his arm around her. "Are you all right?"

"That was Gloria. She begged me to come back to work, because there are too many details regarding the picnic and no one knows what to do. She said that the Lord gave me the vision and no one else."

"I agree. Now do you believe how important you are?"

She rested her head on his chest as she cried. He never felt more important than holding this woman while her tears dampened his shirt.

The large pink lilies filled her office with a sweet fragrance and created a constant distraction. Not so much because of the lovely aroma, but because they were a gift from Seth. She'd stepped into the church this morning to a welcome of cheers and applause and hugs. Their words of encouragement and support had chased away her lingering doubts about returning to work. Now she knew what it was like to have people who cared. Until now there'd only been Mavis, but now she had the church staff. And Jack and Seth.

Right now, though, she had a lot of catching up to do. The picnic was only four days away. Thankfully her organization skills allowed her to quickly get on top of things and back on track. She loved her job, loved the people she worked with, and she wanted this anniversary picnic to meet all expectations.

She inhaled the heady fragrance of the floral arrangement again, unable to keep from smiling as she looked at them. She'd had to clear a special spot on her desk to set them. But it was the card and sentiment written on it that kept encroaching into her thoughts. "Welcome back to work, Sunshine. You are amazing and I know this picnic will prove that to everyone. Love, Seth."

It was the words *Love, Seth* that had her heart speeding up and putting a perpetual smile on her lips. She'd called him, and the sound of his deep voice and the affection in his tone changed her insides to warm honey.

She had to be careful, though. Her heart told her she loved him, but her head was still reluctant to admit it. She wanted to be sure, and she wanted all the shadows of the past chased away first. She'd told him everything, but they hadn't had a chance to work through it. She'd placed that on her list of things to do after the picnic. This event required all her attention, though how she was supposed to work with the heady scent of the lilies and the memory of Seth's caringtone ringing in her ears she didn't know.

With great effort she forced her attention back to the picnic checklist—finalizing paperwork, double-checking vendors and putting out small fires along the way. When the phone rang she sent up a prayer that it wasn't another problem. Unfortunately, it was a big one.

She ended the call, then rested her head in her hands and searched for a solution. Without a second thought, she picked up her cell and called Seth, launching into her story the moment he answered. "Do you have a second? You won't believe what's happened. Vern Bailey crashed his plane."

"What? When? Is he all right?"

"He's fine, just a few scratches. He took it up this morning, but when he landed he blew a tire and skidded off the runway, and it flipped over. There's no way he can get it repaired and here for the picnic. I don't know what I'm going to do. Everyone is counting on seeing that old airplane."

"I know. Myself included."

"I wish I could put something else in that spot, but there's not enough time to find another pilot willing to haul his plane down here for a day."

"How about a police car?"

"What do you mean?"

"The department has a community liaison car. It's a standard police cruiser with all the markings, but it's not a response vehicle. We use it for making appearances at community events. The kids can sit in it, flash the lights and sound a modified siren. There'll be an officer there to explain everything and answer questions."

"That would be wonderful. Do you think you can do that?"

"Sure. I'll set it up. The only problem I see is that it's too late to change your flyers and other notifications."

"No problem. I'll put it up on the website and ask everyone to spread the word. I think a police car is a pretty good substitute for an old airplane. Thank you. You've become an invaluable assistant. You're like a hero who sweeps in and saves the day."

"I'm here whenever you need me, Sunshine. I like assisting you. And I'd like to be your hero."

His words kept her mood soft and mushy the rest of the day. It grew even warmer when she received his text telling her the arrangements for the liaison car were all set. He added a personal message at the end: You're doing great, Sunshine. This is going to be a super picnic.

He'd added a thumbs-up emoji and a smiley with hearts for eyes. His words of encouragement warmed her from within, lifting another layer from the dark despair she'd been mired in since her arrest.

With the exception of Mavis, no one had ever believed in her or trusted her this much. Even after her past had been exposed, Seth was still there, stepping up to be her hero. Dare she hope that there might be a future for them, after all? Could he overcome what she'd done and consider a future together?

It didn't seem likely, but for now she'd let herself dream. Surely the worst was over. What could possibly happen now?

Seth hurried inside his house Saturday morning. He'd been up at the crack of dawn helping set things up for the picnic today. The bouncy houses were in position and being inflated. Amos had delivered the ponies, and had them fed and secured to the sweep ready to greet the children. Phil had volunteered to handle the first shift at the liaison car. And the vendors were all setting up. Carrie's fears about the weather hadn't materialized, and the day was warm, sunny and perfect for a day at the park.

After a quick shower, he dressed quickly in jeans and a dark navy blue Dover PD T-shirt. He was officially on duty today, but since he was working security his boss thought a full uniform might dampen the mood. The T-shirt would let people know in a more subtle way the police were on the premises.

Jack had spent the night at Seth's mom's, and she planned on taking him to the picnic sometime today. A quick glance at his watch told him he had to get a move on. He was due at the park in ten minutes and he anticipated a lot of traffic despite the shuttle service.

A noise from the front porch reminded him the postman had arrived. He retrieved the mail and sorted through the stack. One envelope stopped his heart. The DNA lab. Inside was the answer he'd been waiting for. He found himself unable to tear it open. What if it proved Jack wasn't his?

How would he go on without that little boy in his life? But what if it proved Jack *was* his son? Then he could start planning the rest of his life. A bigger house for Jack, a college fund—a mother.

He was getting ahead of himself. Fear was paralyzing his ability to make a decision. If he opened the envelope now and it was bad news, it would weigh on him throughout the entire picnic. He didn't want to ruin Carrie's big moment, but if he waited until later, he'd be equally distracted by the nagging doubts.

Maybe there was a middle ground. Carrie would be as anxious to see the results of the test as he was. Maybe they should open it together. That way they could either celebrate or comfort each other if the news was bad. They'd started this journey with Jack together, and it was only right that they end it the same way. Besides, he wanted her to be with him when he learned the truth.

Slipping the envelope into his jeans, he locked up and climbed into his truck. He'd tell Carrie about the letter and they'd open it together when the picnic was over.

The park was already filling up when he pulled into the last available slot in the parking lot. In a short while the nearby streets would be lined with vehicles, and the shuttles would be chugging back and forth from downtown.

He found Carrie in the pavilion where the band was setting up. She turned when he called her name, and her smile brightened the already sunny sky. A playful breeze made her blond hair flutter. In the pink slacks and floral top she wore today she looked like a walking flower garden. She truly was a ray of sunshine. And she brought a light into his life he'd never expected.

"Officer Montgomery reporting for duty. How's it going here?"

"This is the last thing to set up. Then it's just a matter of keeping things running smoothly."

He touched her arm, craving the contact. "I saw Ralph. He's in high cotton as the greeter. It gives him an excuse to tell all his stories."

"I knew he'd be perfect for that."

Seth took her hand and guided her from the pavilion toward the cul-de-sac, stopping under the sheltering limbs of an old live oak dripping with Spanish moss. "I need to show you something." He pulled the envelope from his pocket and handed it to her.

Her eyes widened. "The test results. Is Jack yours?"

He pointed to the seal. "I haven't opened it yet."

"Why not?"

He took the envelope from her and slipped it back into his pocket. "I wanted to do it together. You've been a part of this journey with Jack from the very beginning. You deserve to be part of the answer. I thought I could meet you at your house after the picnic is all done and we'll open it together."

"What about Jack. Shouldn't he be there, too?"

"Yeah. If the test is positive I want him to know right away. If not, then I'll do whatever it takes to make him mine. He needs to know that, too."

Someone shouted to Carrie and she waved. "I'd better see what that's about." She stood on tiptoe and kissed his cheek. "Thank you for wanting me to be with you when you learn the truth. That means a lot to me."

Seth watched her walk away, her every movement light and feminine and full of life. He'd never met anyone like her and he was determined to make her a part of his future. But right now it was time to patrol the park. There were other officers here, but with this many people in one place, you couldn't be too cautious.

"Hey, Seth."

Phil waved him over to the liaison car. A couple of elderly men were checking it out. Seth acknowledged them with a friendly nod. "How's it going? Is it drawing a crowd?"

"Not bad, and it's early yet." Phil shifted his weight and glanced away as if preparing to discuss something important. "You and Carrie make a nice couple. It's not hard to see you two are crazy about each other."

Seth frowned at the change in the man's attitude. "And?"

"And I hope I find that kind of relationship someday."

The longing in Phil's tone softened Seth's irritation. "Let me give you a little advice. Make sure you're looking in the right place and for the right woman. Look beyond the packaging to the person inside. If you don't, you'll never find what you're looking for."

The day passed so quickly Carrie barely had time to catch her breath, though she'd taken a break when Jack arrived. She had watched him ride the ponies and play in the bouncy house. Seth had helped him play a few carnival games, they'd eaten way too much junk food and they'd had an enjoyable time together. Now twilight was settling in. The park closed at dark, which meant the picnic would be shutting down soon. She'd made arrangements to pick up Jack from Francie's as soon as she was done at the park. Seth had volunteered to be the last man out and make sure the park was secured. He would come by her place as soon as he was finished, and they'd open the envelope and learn once and for all if he was Jack's biological father.

At the end of the day Carrie had overcome all of her lingering anxiety about the residents of Dover harboring ill will toward her over the laptops. A few people gave her harsh looks and one or two even made snide remarks, but for the most part it was if the incident had never happened. Her hope had been renewed that she could remain in Dover, after all.

More importantly, the picnic had been all she'd hoped. Everyone had had a good time, and no major issues had arisen. All the vendors had shown up, and all the volunteers had worked like troupers. The games had been a hit, and the pony rides were the most popular attraction. Even the last-minute substitution of a police car for the airplane had gone well. The kids had flocked to it filled with questions. There'd been plenty of food and drink to feed the large crowd. The food donations had exceeded their expectations, as well. Seth's brother Linc had told her they'd packed their van to the ceiling, and both Martha's House and the local homeless shelter would have their cupboards stocked for a long time.

She glanced into the backseat of her car at Jack, who was playing quietly with his little cars. In a short while the question of his parentage would be answered. She believed with every fiber of her being that the test would prove Seth was his father. She was convinced that the Lord had brought them together because they were meant to be a family.

As for her family, Neil hadn't been heard from in over a week. She'd started to believe he'd given up and found another way to get his money.

Carrie pulled her car to a stop beneath her carport, relieved to be home again. Jack had learned to unfasten his seat belt and was ready to pop out of the car the moment she opened the door. He raced up the walk to the back door, bouncing on his toes, eager to get inside and see Leo. She marveled at the child's energy.

Carrie unlocked her back door, but before she could open it all the way Jack pushed through and shouted for Leo. The dog met him in the middle of the kitchen and the pair began a wrestling match, eliciting giggles from the boy and a wagging tail from the dog.

Her cheery kitchen welcomed her home, easing the last of her fatigue and allowing a sense of satisfaction to take root. She was exhausted but exhilarated. The picnic had been a bigger success than she'd ever dreamed. The turnout had been phenomenal, too. She wouldn't be surprised if nearly every resident of Dover had put in an appearance. She pulled her phone from her purse. Seth had promised to text her when he was on his way to the house and she didn't want to miss it.

She had felt guilty about leaving when there was still plenty of cleanup to do, but Seth was right. She couldn't do it all and the cleanup crew would do a good job. Ralph had even volunteered. She hoped Seth would keep an eye on him. He'd worked hard today greeting everyone, answering questions and giving directions. His special kind of warmth and friendliness had added so much to the entire event.

"Miss Carrie, can I have a cookie?"

"Just one. You've had a lot of sweets today." Jack hurried to the counter, his fingers clutching the edge, his eyes bright with anticipation as she lifted the lid from the cookie jar and handed him one. "They're almost gone. We'll have to bake more tomorrow."

"Isn't that sweet? You not only have a boyfriend who's a cop, but you're making cookies for his kid."

Carrie whirled around at the sound of Neil's voice. He stood in the doorway, the sneer on his face telling her he'd been drinking. It always brought out the nasty in him. "Get out. Seth will be here any minute and he'll have you arrested."

Neil let out a harsh laugh. "Like he arrested you?"

"I can't help you, Neil. I don't have any money to give you."

"No, but your boyfriend does. I saw that big old house his family lives in. They have plenty of money and they'll pay to get you and the kid back safely."

Carrie's blood froze in her veins. When she had seen Neil in the park that day, he had probably followed her to the Montgomerys, too. "They aren't rich. Not like you think."

Neil lunged forward and grabbed her arm. "Let's go. I've got a nice cozy place for you and the kid to wait."

Frantic, she tried to think of a way to let Jack get

away or hide, but it was too late. The only way out now was right past her brother. She took Jack's hand, wrapping the other around his shoulders and holding him close to her side. Slowly she moved forward, snatching up both their jackets and using the movement to hide her phone in the folds. Later she could slip it into her pants pocket. Maybe Neil wouldn't think to ask for it and she could get help.

"Hurry up."

Leo started to follow, but Neil shouted at the dog and he scurried away. Neil motioned them to the door. Carrie was glad he didn't have a gun, though she wouldn't put it past him. She had to find a way to let Seth know they were in danger.

She stopped and glanced at Neil. "I'd better turn out the lights. If I leave them on people will get curious and check on me."

"Hurry up. Leave the boy here. Just make sure you don't try anything funny."

Carrie moved quickly, slapping switches and casting the house into darkness. Her stomach spun, but she ignored it. In the kitchen she hurried to Jack's side and lifted him into her arms, hitting the last switch as Neil shoved her out the door.

She prayed that Seth would understand the message she'd left him. If not, she feared for her and Jack's safety. Neil was desperate for money, and in his current state he was capable of anything.

Chapter Eleven

Seth pulled out of the parking lot, buoyed by a sense of satisfaction. The park was clean and secure. The only signs of the big day were the worn patches of grass where the booths had stood and a bare circular path under the trees where the ponies had been. The parks department would take care of replacing the sod and restoring the grounds.

A flutter of nervous excitement put a smile on his face. The Dover anniversary picnic had been a big success, and somewhere during the day he'd realized that Carrie was the woman he wanted to spend his life with. He'd known he was in love with her, but seeing her manage all the venues with the skill of a puppeteer—tweaking this, adjusting that, troubleshooting every detail—had deepened his admiration for her strength and caring. Watching her with Jack had sealed the deal. Any doubts or reservations had vanished. She loved Jack as much as he did. Possibly more.

Something deep inside had settled into place after

being off-kilter for a long time. For the first time in his life he felt he knew the meaning of contentment. That edgy, trapped feeling he'd had growing up, his deep fear that he'd never be satisfied anywhere, was gone. Having Jack and Carrie in his life filled every molecule of his body with a peace and joy greater than anything he'd ever known. He thanked the Lord for this blessing. He'd taken a long, meandering journey to find where he belonged, but he'd found it and he was determined to convince Carrie that she should be part of his future.

Parked in his drive a few minutes later, he slipped the DNA-lab envelope from his pocket. He was anxious to open it with Carrie and learn for certain what his soul already knew. Jack was his. Even if the test was negative, he knew the Lord had brought the boy into his life to be his son, and he'd do whatever it took to make it legal. And it was time to tell Carrie how much he loved her. He knew she had feelings for him, but her past still held her captive. He prayed she was ready to let him come alongside her, and they'd battle that together.

He checked his phone. He'd texted Carrie when he'd left the park. She usually responded right away, but she hadn't. Climbing out of the car, he mentally replayed the speech he planned on giving to Carrie. He crossed to the gate in her yard and stepped through, glancing at the house. He stopped. Something wasn't right. It took him a second to realize the lights were all out. Carrie's house was never dark. Ever. Even when she wasn't home there were low-wattage lights illuminating the windows.

Fear lanced through his chest. Something was wrong.

As he approached the back door, he noticed it was ajar. His gut kicked. Cautiously he stepped inside, calling her name. The lack of light only amped up his alarm. His pulse raced and all his senses were on alert. He wished he had his gun, but his role at the park hadn't required it. Only the uniformed officers had carried their weapons. A quick search of the cottage revealed a broken cookie on the kitchen floor and Carrie's purse on the chair. He could only think of one reason Carrie would leave her purse and turn off her lights. She was trying to send him a message. And it wasn't good. But where were they and what had happened?

Back in the kitchen, he scanned the room again and saw the paper on the table. He snatched it up, his entire body turning to ice as he read. Neil had taken Carrie and Jack and he wanted fifty-thousand dollars for their return. He wanted it delivered in two hours to the burned-out store on the edge of town. Fear closed his throat. His family didn't have access to that kind of money.

He crumpled the note in his fist. Carrie had left the lights off as a signal.

He reported the kidnapping, then called Phil. He'd been following up on any leads that involved Neil. Seth prayed Phil had found something in his investigation that would lead them to Carrie and Jack.

"He came back to town yesterday evening, but I only learned about it this afternoon." As Phil caught him up, Seth paced. "We figured his partner was the one who took the laptops and put them in Carrie's car. Gloria identified him as a man who had come to the church inquiring about becoming a member and requested a tour of the campus. We figure Neil was in the vicinity, waiting to make his anonymous call as soon as the laptops were reported missing. He wanted to make sure Carrie was nabbed for the theft."

"What about now? Do you have any idea where he might have taken Carrie and Jack?"

"Not yet. Though we did get a complaint about someone trespassing at an old farmhouse out on Post Oak Road."

"Has anyone checked it out?"

"Not yet."

"Then I'll start there. Oh, and put a trace on Carrie's phone."

"Seth, you can't go charging in there without backup, and without knowing for sure they're there. You could get them both killed. Get your hard head to the station and let Captain Durrant take the lead."

Seth knew Phil was right. If Carrie and Jack were at the old farm and he went in unprepared, he could make things worse. If they weren't there, then he'd wasted valuable time. Common sense waged a fierce battle with his emotions as he steered his cruiser toward the police station. The officer in him knew he was doing the right thing, but his heart wanted to turn the car around and take the highway directly toward Post Oak Road.

Seth began a constant prayer for the safe rescue of Carrie and Jack. When he saw Carrie again, he'd tell her how he felt and not waste any more time. And if he ever got his hands on Neil Overton... He swallowed the bitter taste of anger and gripped the steering wheel with white knuckles. He had to find them.

They were his family.

Carrie held Jack on her lap as Neil drove his dilapidated car down a dark country road. She'd tried to talk to him several times, but he'd ignored her or told her to shut up. Jack buried his head in her chest, and she patted his back. It was the only encouragement she could offer at the moment.

She stole a glance at her brother. She didn't know the man he'd become. Neil had always been stern and serious, but somewhere along the line he'd become angry and nasty. "Why are you doing this, Neil?"

"Told you. I need to get out of the country. That takes money. You refused to help, but I'm sure your boyfriend will be more cooperative. He has more incentive than you did."

"Neil you don't—"

He held up his fist to silence her. She pulled Jack a little closer, praying for safety and deliverance from this volatile situation. She prayed for Seth to find them quickly and she prayed for courage.

The car slowed and veered off the road onto a deeply rutted driveway between overhanging trees. When they pulled into the open, she saw the shadow of an old farmhouse. One window held a faint glow of light. She had no idea where they were or how far out of town they'd come. Her fingers wrapped around the phone in her pants pocket. If she could just get a text—even a partial one—sent to Seth, then he could track them down.

Neil stopped the car, got out and came around to her door. He grabbed her arm and she struggled to hold on to Jack as her brother forced them across the uneven ground.

The front door of the house opened and a man stepped onto the porch. "Where you going to put them?"

Neil laughed and shoved her forward. "I got the perfect place."

It took a moment for Carrie's eyes to adjust to the dark as they walked beyond the house and toward the trees. She made out the shape of a small shed, its roof sloped or sagging, she couldn't tell which. What she did know was that Neil intended to lock them inside the cramped old shack. Terror clamped like icy fingers around her throat making it hard to breathe.

Please, Lord, don't let him put me inside there. Please let there be a light. Please don't leave me in the dark.

The opening strains of the *Downton Abbey* theme song split the silence. Her phone. She cringed. She should have turned the phone to silent. Neil cursed, jerked her to a halt and rammed his hand into her pocket. He spewed a string of ugly words, then dropped the phone and stomped on it.

Jack shivered against her.

Neil shoved her inside. The wooden door slammed behind her with a dreadful finality. Cold sweat covered her skin. Pounding on the door, she screamed her brother's name.

"Miss Carrie, I'm scared."

Jack's trembling voice broke through her rising

panic. She couldn't let her fears control her. She wanted to curl up in a ball and cry the way she had when she was a kid and Neil had locked her in that closet. She'd remained in the fetal position, crying for hours, until Neil had decided to return home and let her out. She'd found a place to go in her mind that had allowed her to endure the dark. She didn't have that luxury now—Jack needed her.

"I know you're scared. I am, too." She pressed him close to her side, trying desperately to see in the inky blackness. She remembered noticing a bench when they were shoved inside. At least they wouldn't have to sit on the floor, though she had no idea where it was. There were cracks in the walls so they wouldn't suffocate. She could feel the walls, look for a loose board, but that would mean moving around in this dark space. She shivered. She didn't want to think about what might be lurking in the old shed. Spiders, snakes, rodents. Fear pulled a gasp from her throat, which in turn made Jack grasp her more tightly.

Somehow she had to set aside her own terror to make Jack feel safe. Forcing a calming breath into her lungs, she reached out and felt the door, then slowly turned and took a few steps forward, feeling for the bench. Hands outstretched, she prayed she'd come in contact with something solid and not an icky spiderweb. After three cautious steps, her knee hit something hard and her hand landed on the wall. She was grateful that all she felt was the rough, weathered wood. She brushed the seat of the bench, making sure it was empty, pushing aside a metal object on the end before sitting down and pulling Jack up beside her. "There. Now we'll wait for Seth to come and find us."

"I want my daddy."

Carrie's heart melted. They'd never gotten the chance to open the letter with the DNA results, but Jack had claimed Seth as his father. Seth would be so happy.

They should have been celebrating right now. She'd envisioned a happy party with special cupcakes for the occasion. If the news was negative she had planned on calling them consolation cupcakes.

Carrie opened her eyes. The darkness tightened her throat. The fierce need to escape overtook her mind and her breath came rapidly.

"Is Daddy coming?"

Jack. She had to think of him first and keep him feeling safe. "I know he is. It just might take a while for him to find us."

"Will he bust open the door?"

She hugged him close. "He might."

"Superman busts through doors."

Carrie continued the game, hoping to downplay their situation. "Maybe he'll come in the window." There weren't any windows but she chose to ignore that.

"I hope he drops through the roof on a rope. That would be way cool."

"Just like in the movies."

"My dad catches bad guys, and locks them up and makes 'em go away, doesn't he?"

"That's right, but we'll have to be brave until he shows up, okay?" She prayed Jack's words would come true.

"Miss Carrie, I'm scared."

She shifted him into her lap and held him close to her heart. "I know, sweetheart. But Jesus will watch over us. He's promised to never forsake us."

"What's does that mean?"

"He'll stay right beside us in this dark place until your daddy comes to take us home."

"I can't see him."

"No, but if you close your eyes and talk to him, he'll hear you."

Jack relaxed in her arms and she prayed again for their safety. For strength and courage to keep her undercurrent of panic from rising to the surface. She prayed for wisdom to keep Jack from becoming too frightened. She knew firsthand that fear was a contagious emotion. If she grew fearful and gave in to it, Jack would be swept along with her. *Please, Lord, show me You're here.*

She opened her eyes, her gaze drawn to a sliver of light. Was she imagining it? Was she seeing things now? She shut her eyes and opened them again. It was still there. A thread of light from somewhere outside the shed. A floodlight? Light from the house? Whatever the source, it was the thread of hope she needed to keep her sanity. The shed was still filled with suffocating darkness. With each breath she inhaled dust and mold and who knows what else. The smell of dirt, rotted wood and oil clung to her nose. The bench beneath them was dirty and splintered, but that one filament of light gave her the strength to keep her own fears tamped down.

"I want Barky."

"I know. But he's nice and warm at the house. He'd be awfully cold out here with us."

She held Jack closer, fixing her gaze on the crack of light like a lifeline. A verse came to mind. One so appropriate it stole her breath. "'We walk by faith not by sight.'"

There was no way out of the ramshackle shed, and she had no idea of what was beside her or above her. All she had was the determination to protect Jack, the trust that Seth would find them and the assurance that the Lord would be with them.

Seth stood on the sidelines watching as Neil's cohort, Stan Richards, was escorted to a patrol car. Thanks to a coordinated effort, they'd nabbed Richards when he'd stepped out of the shadows to pick up the bag full of money, which was actually cut-up newsprint. Unfortunately, he had refused to tell them where Neil was or where Carrie and Jack might be.

Seth grew more and more irritated the longer he stalled. He was a newbie on the force and had no authority to even question the guy. But fear for his family was building rapidly, threatening to explode.

His hopes rose when he saw Phil jogging toward him.

"They spotted Neil's car at that old farm. He's inside. They're waiting for backup." He grinned. "You and me, pal."

Seth sat in the passenger seat of the cruiser as Phil sped away from the drop site. They were traveling at a good clip, but it felt like forever until they reached the farm. They met up with the other officers and sheriff's deputies and were updated on the situation and the plan to capture Neil.

Every nerve in Seth's body screamed to charge in, take out Neil and find Carrie and Jack. Being forced to stand by and wait was driving him crazy. He tried not to think about all that could go wrong. Hopefully, they could avoid gunfire, but there was no guarantee. If all went well, they'd surround the house, capture Neil, then rescue Carrie and Jack. His greatest fear was that her brother had locked her in the dark again. He'd seen the stark fear in her eyes the night the lights went out. Jack would be scared, too, but if Carrie lost it… He didn't want to think what that might do to his son.

And Jack was his son. He'd promised Carrie they'd open the envelope together, but with Jack missing, Seth needed to know the truth. The DNA test proved what he'd already known in his heart: Jack was his biological son.

Time to move. The officers advanced. He and Phil held their position. It was over in moments. Shots were fired, but no one was hurt. Seth pushed through, grabbed Neil by the shirt and yanked him up. The officers escorting him pushed Seth back.

"Where are they? What have you done with them?"

Neil's shoulders sagged and he jerked his head to the left. "That shed."

Seth could barely make out the shape of a tiny building nestled in the shade of overgrown trees. And it was dark as pitch. He broke into a run.

* * *

Jack had dozed off. Poor guy was exhausted from the picnic and now this. She had no idea how long they'd been in the shed. It could have been a few minutes or an hour. There was no way of gauging the passage of time by the noises outside. Their only company were the crickets and the owls. Every now and then she'd catch a hint of rustling outside, but she couldn't tell if it was the breeze moving through the trees or an animal in the brush.

The silence closed in around her and she started to hum. Keeping her mind occupied was imperative to controlling the fear. She felt Jack lift his head up. She stoked his hair. "Do you know the song 'Zacchaeus Was a Wee Little Man'?" He shook his head against her chest. "It's easy. I'll teach it to you." Softly she began to sing the Sunday-school song. Jack joined in the second time around. When he grew silent, she gently rocked him, drawing comfort herself from the motion. She was managing to maintain her emotional balance, but she wouldn't be able to forever.

"Miss Carrie, are you scared?"

She wasn't sure how to answer. "Yes, Jack. I am."

He wiggled in her lap and she heard the clink of little cars in his pocket. "You can hold one of my cars, then you won't be so scared."

Her love for the child deepened tenfold. He had the same caring heart as his father. She fumbled a bit until she found his little hand and took the small toy. "Thank you, Jack. I feel better already."

A shout from outside shattered the stillness. She

froze. More shouts. Pounding. A commotion. Shots fired. She lowered her head and held Jack. Had Seth come to rescue them or was Neil causing the disturbance?

"Is Daddy coming?"

She hushed him and prayed.

Pounding on the door chilled her blood. Had Neil come for them again? To let them go or... She refused to think of the ugly possibilities.

"Carrie? Are you in there?"

"Seth! Yes, we're here."

The shed shook as someone pounded the door. It splintered and burst open, and she shielded her eyes. When she looked she saw Seth coming toward her. Her entire body sagged in relief.

"Daddy!" Jack shifted in her lap as Seth picked him up and held him close.

"You okay, buddy?"

Carrie surfed an emotional swell of relief. Seth took her arm, urging her to her feet and into his embrace. She shared it with Jack and it felt so right, the three of them clinging to one another.

"Let's get you out of here."

Carrie stood beside the paramedic unit watching Seth and Jack. They were a sight to behold. Jack had wrapped his little arms around Seth's neck and hadn't budged. Even when the EMTs checked him out, he refused to let go.

The sight warmed her to the core and also left her with a familiar sense of exclusion. She didn't really belong with them. She was a friend, a convenient babysitter. She knew Seth had developed feelings for her—his kiss had told her that. His pet name, too. But tonight changed everything. Her brother had kidnapped his child and it was her fault. Unintentionally, perhaps, but still, Neil was her family.

Once the relief of finding his son safe had passed, Seth would start to realize that associating with her wasn't something he wanted for Jack. She couldn't blame him.

Stepping away, she caught sight of the shed, her gaze searching the darkness. She squinted and looked closer. In the distance, barely visible between the trees, a light shone. Probably a floodlight from a neighboring farm. She smiled and lifted up a thankful prayer. No one would have noticed the light. Its glow was too weak to penetrate the dense woods, but it had been positioned perfectly in line with the crack in the shed wall to illuminate her hope and give her the reassurance she needed. The Lord had indeed been with them. He always was and always would be.

She spun around when Seth called her name. "You ready to go home?"

She nodded. More than ready. The adrenaline sustaining her for the last few hours was fading and fatigue was setting in. As she settled into the dark sedan, the patrol car carrying her brother passed by and she caught a glimpse of him. A sense of sadness rose up from somewhere long ago. He'd been a decent man at one point. Maybe he could be again. She made a vow to pray for him.

She must have dozed off on the ride home because when she opened her eyes, Seth was pulling to a stop in his driveway. He reached over and took her hand, giving it a squeeze. "Would you mind coming inside while I get Jack ready for bed? I want to talk to you."

"Okay. I'm not ready to be alone right now, anyway."

Carrie strolled through the house toward the front windows. She was tired, but too keyed up from the day to truly relax. She was glad Seth had invited her in. Being close to him and Jack gave her comfort and direction. Once she went home, she knew her thoughts would roll and tumble back over the day, her old insecurities would rush out and she'd be fortunate if she slept at all.

She glanced over her shoulder when she heard footsteps in the hall. Seth was walking behind a very sleepy pajama-clad boy. Jack hurried forward and climbed into her lap, resting his head on her chest.

"I love you, Miss Carrie. Thank you for making me not scared."

Tears stung her eyes. "Oh, Jack, you were the bravest boy I've ever known. You helped me, too."

"Daddy saved us, didn't he?"

She glanced at Seth who was beaming with happiness. "Yes, he did."

Seth sat down onto the coffee table holding her gaze. "I wanted to tell you that I opened the envelope with the test results. I know we were going to open it together, but when you and Jack were missing, I had to know the truth."

She held her breath. "And?"

"He's my son." He reached out and smoothed his palm over the boy's hair.

Jack smiled, his cobalt eyes bright with joy. "He's my real daddy forever and ever, and I don't have to go away and I'm getting a puppy."

Carried laughed and placed a kiss on his cheek. "I'm so glad, Jack." She shifted her gaze to Seth's handsome face. "For both of you."

"Come on, buddy. Bedtime."

Jack gave her a hug, then padded off with his dad to bed. Carrie's heart bloomed with joy. Seth could move forward now, secure in the knowledge that no one could ever take Jack away. The boy would know a life of unconditional love and security. Seth would make sure of that.

"I'm sorry."

She glanced up at Seth as he returned. "For what?"

He reached for her, pulling her to her feet and into his arms. "For not waiting to open the test results together. I know you were looking forward to it."

She touched his jaw, the normally clean-shaven skin now rough with day-end stubble. "All that matters is that it proved you're Jack's father. Was he happy?"

A small chuckle accompanied the nod. "He nearly choked me with a hug."

"He started calling you Daddy while we were in the shed. I think he's always known, the same way you did."

Seth placed his hands on the sides of her face, his thumbs gently caressing her cheeks. "I was so worried. I thought I might lose you both. When I saw that shed and how dark it was, I kept thinking how terrified you must be. I'm sorry I couldn't get to you sooner."

"No. You arrived at the perfect time."

"Are you all right? Really?"

"I'm going to be." He looked into her eyes and she saw his dark eyes soften.

"I don't want to lose you." He drew her closer, holding her against his chest like a precious possession. Slowly he shifted, lifting her chin with a gentle touch of his fingers. His lips found hers and she melted against him, aware of the pounding of his heart in time with hers. The terror of the day drained away, and it was replaced with a sense of belonging and connection that she'd craved her whole life.

When he ended the kiss, he continued to hold her as if afraid to let her go. His concern touched her deeply. "I'm fine. In fact, I faced my fears in that shed and overcame them."

He pulled back. "You're not afraid of the dark now?"

"Not like I was. I doubt I'll ever be completely comfortable in the dark, but it's manageable now. I'm not a slave to it. All I could think about in there was keeping Jack safe. We sang songs and made up stories about how you would come to save us. Jack was convinced you'd bust through the ceiling and come down a rope." Gently she touched the dimple on the side of his mouth. "Mostly I prayed, and the Lord answered me with a teeny sliver of light through the boards. I finally realized I'd spent so much of my life in darkness. Not from lack of light, but from lack of understanding, and faith. God was with us in that shed every minute. I think He allowed me to be there not only to comfort Jack, but to conquer my fears."

"I think He brought you into our lives to love us and to show me the woman I want in my life forever. Carrie, I love you. I have for a while, but I was afraid to take that next step. I made such a mess of my first marriage. You've taught me how to love again, to be happy. You're the most amazing woman I've ever known. Marry me and help me raise my son."

The words were ones she'd never thought she'd hear. Her heart was so full each beat threatened to burst from her rib cage. She'd been worried that he'd turn away from her after what Neil had done. She hadn't expected his confession of love. But did he mean it, or was it merely the emotional aftermath of the adrenaline-filled day? How would he feel after a night's sleep and time to think things through?

She rested her hands on his chest. "It's been a long and difficult day. I don't want to make any important decisions right now. I want to have a clear head. Do you understand?"

"I do." He rested his forehead against hers his arms holding her close. "We'll talk again tomorrow. I do love you, Carrie. That's not going to change by morning." He placed a tender kiss on her mouth before releasing her. "I'll walk you home."

"No. You shouldn't leave Jack even for a second. He might have a nightmare. I'll be fine."

"All the lights are out at your place."

"I know. But I'm not afraid now. I know where all the switches are and I won't be alone."

Seth followed her to the front porch, watching as she crossed to her house and went inside. She switched on the lights, then went to the window. Seth waved. She waved back, then lowered the shade.

Her heart soared. Seth loved her. And though she hadn't told him so, she loved him, too.

She'd realized the moment she looked into his eyes that he'd not only rescued them from Neil's plot, but he'd rescued her from a life without love. How had she ever imagined she could walk through her life caring only for certain people and keeping her heart locked away?

But how could he accept her now? Her secret was out, and her brother would be charged with kidnapping and trying to extort money from Seth's family. He was a lawman. How could he ever accept a woman with a criminal past and a brother who would likely spend the rest of his life in prison?

Chapter Twelve

The aroma of fresh coffee filled Carrie's senses and gave her a jump start on the day. She poured the brew into her favorite mug, and doctored it with sweetener and hazelnut-flavored creamer. The first sip lifted her spirits. She'd slept like a baby, with no bad dreams, no tossing and turning, and only memories of feeling safe and cherished.

Seth loved her. At least he'd said so last night. She wasn't ready to think about how he might feel in the harsh light of day, but she was too happy to let anything negative enter her mind.

Glancing out the front window, the colorful bushes in the park across the way beckoned her out into the morning sunshine. She settled onto the porch swing, her gaze lifting to the blue sky streaked with golden rays from the sun. She had so much to be thankful for—her deliverance from danger and her fear of the dark, and a future filled with endless possibilities.

And Seth's love. He'd nicknamed her Sunshine because of her blond hair and sky blue eyes. He said her smile reminded him of summer. What would he say if she told him that every time she looked at him, he filled her heart with warmth and sunshine, too?

The ringtone on her cell drew her gaze to the screen. Mavis. Carrie took the call eagerly. "I was going to call you in a few minutes."

"How are you this morning? No ill effects from your ordeal?"

She'd called Mavis last night before turning in, partly needing to hear her friend's voice and seeking reassurance, but also to share that the Lord had delivered her from her lifelong fear. "I'm feeling good, considering. Better than I ever imagined."

"Being set free will do that for you."

"I'm finding that out."

"So, are you going to tell me the rest? What about Seth? I know you left a lot out of our talk last night."

Carrie didn't bother to pretend she didn't know what her friend was asking. Mavis knew her better than anyone. "He asked me to marry him."

"I suspected as much. So…what did you say?"

"Nothing. We were too tired, too mentally drained from everything to think clearly."

"And now your insecurities are back, so you can avoid making a decision."

She cringed as the truth hit home. "No. I just want to be sure that what we feel is the real thing, and not because of all the emotions from the kidnapping and rescue."

"Carrie, don't do this to yourself. I know you love

that young man. And he loves you. Even from here in Arkansas I can read the signs. Jack has brought you together and the three of you can make a new life and a wonderful family."

She made it sound so simple. "My brother kidnapped his son. Every time he looks at me, that's all he'll see. If it wasn't for me, that never would have happened."

"Maybe, but that's not the point. You told me last night that the Lord had delivered you from danger and from your fear of the dark, but this morning you're not trusting Him to give you a happy future. Carrie, we all have to live with the memories of our pasts, but it's not so we'll beat ourselves up with our mistakes, but to remind us of the enormity of His grace. Then we can move forward free and whole."

Tears pooled in Carrie's eyes. She wanted to leave the past behind and step into the future completely open to what the Lord had planned. But she wasn't sure she could. Mavis made her promise to trust that God had put Seth and Jack in her life for a reason.

She'd barely hung up when she heard Jack shout her name from next door. He dashed down the porch steps and raced across the lawn, not stopping until he was in her arms. Seth came at a slower pace, the look in his eyes as he drew near warming her inside with love and affection. He was a compelling, handsome man. Few women could resist his charm, but that's not what she loved most about him. It was his compassion and his eagerness to protect others and to help at all times that endeared her to him.

"Good morning."

The sight of his handsome face made her smile. She loved him so very much. "Looks like Jack is none the worse for wear from last night's adventure."

Seth smiled and shrugged. "Other than sleeping at my side like a little leech all night."

Jack shifted in her lap, a small car clutched in his hand. "I'm going to Grandma's today, and me and Evan are going to go swimming in the pool."

She smoothed the hair back from his forehead. "That sounds like a lot of fun."

"I'll be back as soon as I drop him off. We need to talk, Carrie."

Her pulsed skipped. "I know. I'll be here." Her emotions were on a seesaw as she wondered what he would say. Did he still want to marry her, or was he going to retract his offer?

He touched her cheek with his fingertips. "Don't withdraw, okay? Don't put up fences where they aren't needed."

"Maybe they're guardrails."

"You don't need to be guarded from me. Ever."

His words gave rise to hope. Carrie watched her men return home, then drew her knees up to her chin, sending the swing swaying. She had a lot to think about before Seth returned. And a lot of praying to do.

Seth knocked on the back door of Carrie's house, his nerves vibrating like an electrical current. His whole future depended on Carrie's answer. He had to convince her to trust that he'd be at her side forever.

She came to the door, her smile sending a jolt along

his pulse. She was beautiful, and everything he'd ever wanted or needed. "Coffee still hot?"

She waited while he fixed himself a cup, then they sat at the table. He studied her over the rim of his mug. She was nervous and her blue eyes were wary. "Have you thought about my question?"

"Yes. But it's not a matter of a simple yes or no."

"It *is* that simple. Do you love me?"

"Oh, yes. More than I ever thought possible. But there are other things we need to think about. Our backgrounds are so different, our pasts." She wrung her hands. "My family isn't like yours. I didn't grow up the way you did."

"So what? None of that matters."

"Yes, it does. My brother kidnapped your child. My past is filled with crime. Yours is filled with love and service. What will everyone think if you marry someone like me?"

"Carrie, everything is out in the open now. Both our pasts aren't secrets anymore. What more can they do to us? People in small towns can be harsh and unforgiving, but we'll be old news soon. Something else will come along to stir their need for gossip."

She shook her head.

He searched for another angle to convince her. "You think my family is somehow better than everyone else, that we all lived charmed lives? Not true. When our dad died, it hit each of us hard. In fact it pulled us apart. Linc was left to hold everything together, and he made a huge sacrifice along the way. Gil had a disastrous marriage and had to fight for years to regain custody of Abby. Bethany had her career cut short, and had to find a new life. My mom was a widow earlier than she should have been."

She rubbed her forehead. "I have a record. That hardly makes me suitable to raise Jack."

"You had no choice back then. You were just a kid. I had everything—a nice life, loving family, every advantage—and I tossed it away for nothing. I sold my inheritance, and abandoned my beliefs. It doesn't get any more shameful than that."

"That's different. You came to your senses. You've turned your life around, you have a good job and you're doing right by Jack."

"And you did what was necessary to survive. I made a conscious decision to reject my upbringing for selfish indulgence." He took her hands. "We all feel trapped at times in our lives. We all have choices we regret. You need to forgive yourself."

"Have you forgiven yourself?"

"I have. It took me a while, but yes. I'm good." He took her hand. "We can't change what was, but we can go forward with new purpose and understanding. We both were trying to live down our past. Now we need to build a life as husband and wife and provide a home for Jack. I love you. My family loves you. Jack loves you. What else matters?"

He saw the lingering doubts in her eyes and his heart slowed. Was she really going to turn him down? He searched for another angle, some way to convince her that they were meant to be together. He had one last thing he could do. He prayed it would tip the scales in his favor.

"Come with me. I want to show you something."

"Seth."

He refused to let her resist. "Please. It won't take long."

Inside the truck she kept silent. His nerves tensed and his chest tightened as they drove out of town. She didn't speak until he pulled off the road onto a rutted dirt driveway overgrown by brush and twigs.

"Where are we going?"

"You'll like it, I promise. We're almost there."

"I never asked you how you found us."

Seth gave her a quick rundown. He gripped the steering wheel as the memories of last night flared. "When Neil told me where he'd put you, all I could think about was how terrified you must be in the dark. I was out of my mind with worry. I'd rather face a man with a loaded gun than stand by helplessly when you needed me."

Carrie stretched out her hand and he took it in his. "I never doubted you'd rescue us."

The trees opened up and he drove the truck to the edge of the wide stream and stopped.

He could sense her curiosity. He got out and went around to her door. She allowed him to take her hand and they strolled toward the water.

"What is this place?"

"My land."

Her eyes narrowed. "But didn't you sell it to go to Vegas?"

"That's what I thought. But my mom, being the wise woman she is, figured I'd come to my senses one day and regret letting it go. So she mortgaged her business, and had Dad tell me the money was from the sale. I always wondered why the amount was so low. I thought the land would be worth much more. But this is all still mine. And it's where I want to build a home for my family." He watched the light bloom in her blue eyes.

"Oh, this would be a perfect place. I can see a big house up on that rise with a wraparound porch so you see the water and the fields out there, and lots of rocking chairs. And a porch swing." She spun around. "And a tree house in that big oak for Jack. With a zip line. He'd love it here."

She faced him, her whole being aglow with happiness. He took her hands and pulled her close. "Marry me and you can build any kind of house you want." He kissed her softly. "I want to give you all the things you never had. Family, security, love. I want you to have the roots you longed for. I want to be the one who chases away the darkness, and I want to be the one to love you forever."

"Are you sure?"

"I never thought I'd marry again. I'd messed up and I didn't believe I deserved a happily-ever-after. Then Jack showed up and you came into my life and everything changed. I've found what I've always wanted. You. The Lord took my messed-up past and worked it out for good. We were both held captive by our pasts, yet He cleared the way for us. Mom restored my land and the Lord restored our lives." He shrugged. "Besides, my mom told me to marry you. She's convinced you are the one for me."

Gently she touched his cheek. "Your mom is a wise woman. I'd be a fool to ignore her advice."

Hope swelled in his chest. "Is that a yes?"

She nodded. He pulled her close, capturing her mouth with his. She kissed him with no hesitation, no doubts, just the intensity of her love. He drew her closer until he could feel the beating of her heart against his. He was home. Complete. Happy.

He released her, taking her hand, not needing words to express their love. Slowly they walked toward the truck. "I want to tell Mom and Jack as soon as we get back, if that's okay."

"Of course. Do you think he'll be happy?"

"I'm sure of it." He raised her hand to his lips and kissed it. "Which brings up another question. I was wondering, though, how you felt about kids?"

"I love kids. You know that."

"I meant kids of your own."

She pressed closer to his side. "I think I'd like some."

"How many?"

Her eyes twinkled as she smiled at him. "Maybe four or five."

He laughed, then picked her up and swung her around. "Perfect."

Settled in the truck once more, he started the engine and reached for her hand, needing to be in contact. This had to be the happiest day of his life.

Carrie held Seth's hand as they drove back to the Montgomery home, floating on happy emotions. Never had she known such lightness, such exhilaration. All her dreams were coming true.

Francie Montgomery was standing on the porch of her cottage when they pulled up. She waved and came toward them. She must have known, because her smile was wide and her eyes were twinkling as she drew near.

"Something tells me I'm going to have a new daughter-in-law."

Seth nodded. "I finally wore her down."

Carrie searched Francie's expression for reassurance. "I hope that's okay."

Francie placed a hand on Carrie's cheek. "Sweetheart, you make my son and grandson happy. Why wouldn't that be okay?"

Carrie's last concern faded away in the warmth of Francie's gesture. "We wanted to tell Jack as soon as possible."

"Of course." She turned and shouted toward the fort. "Jack! Your dad is here! He has something for you."

A little head appeared above the fort railing. "A puppy?"

Carrie laughed. How she loved that little boy.

"Something better. Come on down."

Jack whizzed down the slide and raced across the yard. Seth picked him up and kissed his cheek. "Did you get me a puppy?"

"Not yet. I thought maybe you'd like something else first. Like a new mom."

Jack frowned and looked at Seth, then Carrie. His mouth gaped open and his eyes widened. "Miss Carrie? Is she going to be my new mom?"

"If it's okay with you."

Jack reached for her, wrapping his arms around her neck as she took him in her arms. "I always wanted a mommy like you."

Tears clogged her throat as she treasured his words. "And I always wanted a little boy like you."

"Can I go tell Evan?"

"Sure."

Jack raced back to the fort. "Evan, Miss Carrie's gonna be my mom!"

"I think our son is happy."

Our son. Two beautiful words.

Seth positioned her to face him. "I think you always knew you'd marry me."

"What do you mean?"

"You named your dog Leo." There was a glint in his cobalt eyes. "Do you know what LEO means in police jargon? Law Enforcement Officer."

Carrie looked at Seth and their gazes meshed. She moved into his strong embrace, sure of where she belonged. Within the caring protection of her lawman, she knew their future would always be filled with love and happiness.

* * * * *

Dear Reader,

Thank you for visiting Dover once again. This time we got to meet the third brother, Seth Montgomery. He's the rebel of the family who escaped small-town life only to learn that the world of excitement he dreamed of was filled with shame and regret. Both Carrie and Seth have pasts that they long to forget, but they both discover it's not that simple.

We all wish we could erase certain events in our pasts, but everything we do, every choice we make, affects others, whether we realize it or not. Seth and Carrie are forced to work together to help little Jack, and in doing so they must overcome their pasts mistakes.

It's so easy to carry our old shame around, taking it out and looking at it, trying to polish it up in hopes of somehow making up for what we've done. But nothing can delete our bad decisions. But the Lord will forget them. To Him it will be like it never happened. Our job is to confess and turn it over to Him. Carrie and Seth were finally able to come to terms with their mistakes and find love and happiness together.

We can't let the past keep a stranglehold on us. Our mistakes should only serve as a reminder of how God's grace is boundless.

Lorraine Beatty

*Can an Amish teacher find love with the Amish fireman
down the road, or will her secret force them apart?*

**Read on for a sneak preview of
HIS AMISH TEACHER,
the next book in Patricia Davids's
heartwarming series, AMISH BACHELORS.**

"We all know Teacher Lillian is a terrible cook, don't we,
children?"

Lillian Keim's students erupted into giggles and some
outright laughter. She crossed her arms and pressed her
lips together to hold back a smile.

Timothy Bowman winked at her to take any sting out
of his comment, but she wasn't offended. They had been
friends for ages and were members of the same Amish
community in Bowmans Crossing, Ohio. She knew he
enjoyed a good joke as well as the next fellow, but he
was deadly serious about his job today and so was she.
The lessons they were presenting might one day prevent
a tragedy.

He stood in front of her class on the infield of the softball
diamond behind the one-room Amish schoolhouse where
she taught all eight grades. Dressed in full fireman's
turnout gear, Timothy made an impressive figure. The
coat and pants added bulk to his slender frame, but he
carried the additional weight with ease. His curly brown

hair was hidden under a yellow helmet instead of his usual straw hat, but his hazel eyes sparkled with mirth. A smile lifted one side of his mouth and deepened the dimples in his tanned cheeks. Timothy smiled a lot. It was one reason she liked him.

His bulky fire coat and pants with bright fluorescent yellow banding weren't Plain clothing, but their Amish church district approved their use because the church elders and the bishop recognized the need for Amish volunteers to help fill the ranks of the local non-Amish fire company. The county fire marshal understood the necessity of special education in the Amish community, where open flames and gas lanterns were used regularly. The Amish didn't allow electricity in their homes. Biannual fire-safety classes were held at all the local Amish schools. This was Timothy's first time giving the class. With Lillian's permission, he was deviating from the normal script with a demonstration outside. Timothy wanted to make an impression on the children. She admired that.

Don't miss
HIS AMISH TEACHER by Patricia Davids,
available March 2017 wherever
Love Inspired® books and ebooks are sold.

www.LoveInspired.com